DISCOVERING TRUTH

MANTLE OF THE GODS

Quest for Truth

Unmasking Truth

Truth Revealed

ANTHOLOGIES

Discovering Truth

DISCOVERING TRUTH

A *MANTLE OF THE GODS* ANTHOLOGY

TRICIA SPARKS

TRINITY GATEWAYS LLC

DISCOVERING TRUTH, A *MANTLE OF THE GODS* ANTHOLOGY

Cover Design by Doris Ross

A Trinity Gateways LLC Publication
www.TrinityGateways.net

ISBN: 0988195186
ISBN-13: 978-0-9881951-8-9

DEDICATIONS

To my parents, you've been my life's compass, showing me my true north.

To Mrs. Dent, my high school English teacher, who took an interest in my writing and put the wind in my sails to pursue my dreams.

To Doris Ross, the captain of my ship. You've been behind me every step pushing me to go further and never give up.

To Lisa Gastineau, my creative partner and crew. You're the one that works behind the scenes and keeps my voyage smooth.

To Dustin, my life's partner on this grand adventure, you make each day brighter because you're in it.

Thank you all for helping me to reach this stop in my journey and I hope that you'll sail with me into the future as well.

PART 1

VOICES FROM THE PAST

1 Monday

"Aloha Kauai the time is 7:52 pm. Your Wildman is winding down as I prepare to head out the door but don't you worry about the night slowing down, we've got a real treat for you tonight; filling in for the lovely Jessica, Queen of Cats, is our own Lady of the Night. She's here to turn up the heat as she takes your requests from eight until midnight."

"That's right Wildman. Prince Charming is out there somewhere but for now I've kicked off the dancing shoes, my feet are up and I'm going to play the tunes to keep you happy until the witching hour. But first, let's start the night off with a song for the city. This one is from me to a special someone out there listening, on behalf of Jessica and Kevin, you know who you are. I hope you like it." the woman purred over the airwaves.

Across town a man sat poised behind the wheel of his Toyota X-Runner frozen, unable to move. He could barely breathe. He knew that voice. It was a sound he could never forget. A ghost from the past and he cursed as the song she'd chosen began to play. It too he knew well "One Way or Another," by Blondie he thought to himself.

His eyes shot to his rear view mirror scanning the area as his lips parted. "Abort mission."

"Vince?" his second questioned with concern in her voice.

He cursed, knowing he couldn't take the command back. "I've been compromised."

"Are you sure? I see no one."

Vince's eyes looked about for indications of a watcher but saw none. "I'm positive, report to base; I'll be back when I'm clear." Vince said before he sped off into the night.

Terra wrapped up her evening broadcast and made her way out toward the lot. The show had been a smash and she smiled. Too bad she couldn't enjoy it. Her nerves were buzzing and she couldn't shake the feeling she was being watched. It had been dogging her since she took the meeting with the station manager about the temp job.

As she approached her sleek, blue, classic 60's, Mustang convertible she felt the hairs on the back of her neck stand on end. She caught the hint of movement reflected in her driver's side mirror and turned to find a Ruger 22 pointed at her head.

Green eyes lit with shock at the sight of him. "You! Vince?" she stared at him dumbfounded unable to believe her eyes. She'd not seen him in five years and… wait he was pointing a gun at her. Her shock faded and anger stirred. "You're behind the hit on Jessica!"

"Me. I'm not the one here that's the assassin." Vince snapped in irritation at the accusation.

"Then what..? Why?"

"I just caught the station broadcast and made my way here to be sure you're not in town to kill me."

Terra laughed bitterly at the notion. "Not everythin I do is about ya Vince."

"You played our song."

"So I'm feeling nostalgic; that doesn't mean I'm after ya. Hell, I didn't even know ya were in town. I stopped lookin for ya in the areas I visit, years ago. I'm a big girl Vince I've moved on."

"Good for you. Now, take out your phone and give your handler, Kieran a call. Tell him the jobs off."

"I don't work for im anymore Vince. I'm not here to kill anyone. I'm here to stop a hit."

"Oh really? That's rich. So, if not Kieran then who is running you now?" Vince asked bitterly.

"No one. I'm retired."

"Retired right. Like you'd retire in the states when you have to know you're on our watch lists."

"Not here. I'm here on a favor."

"Oh, a favor?" he laughed at the word.

"Yes, a friend asked mi ta help out his lady friend."

"Really? Does this friend have a name?"

"Yea. His name is Kevin Hamon. If you want ta, check it out.

He's a cop."

"I will."

"Good."

"If you're on the level, I'll let this go, but you'll owe me."

"Why's that Vince?" Terra asked both amused and annoyed.

"I aborted a mission tonight because I thought I was compromised."

"Really?" she asked trying not to laugh.

"Yeah." Vince answered his nostrils flared and his eyes held anger.

"Good. Now we're even Vince. When ya left, ya nearly got mi killed." Terra muttered before she turned her back to him once more. She opened the car door slipped inside behind the wheel. Terra slammed it in his face; before speeding off into the night.

"That went better than I figured," Vince muttered to himself; before turning and getting in the truck. He punched in the number for the local police station. He was going to look into her Kevin and see if she was telling the truth or if Terra was up to her old tricks again.

"Hello."

"May I speak to a detective Kevin Hamon please?" Vince sat and listened as his call was transferred.

"Detective Hamon."

"Hello detective, my name is Vince; I believe we have a mutual friend, a woman, she goes by the name of Terra Gallagher."

"Yeah, I know Terra.”

"I ran into Terra a few moments ago; she said she was here in town doing you a favor. Is that correct?"

"Look Vince I may know Terra but I don't know you and I'm not comfortable with discussing my business with a total stranger over the phone."

"Fine. Why don't you give Terra a call and we'll arrange a meet. When you're done you can call me back at this number."

"I never got a last name Vince."

"Believe me you won't need it. If you know Terra she'll know who you're talking about." Vince said before he ended the call. He tossed his phone on the seat with disgust. "Damn. She may be on the level." Vince groused before he started up his X-Runner.

As he pulled on to the road; he smirked as he pictured her in his mind. Dark hair blowing in the evening wind as she made her way to her car. "Moved on," he grumbled the words with dislike then laughed. The hell she had. She'd claimed the song was her feeling nostalgic. It was more than that. She was driving his damn car. When he met Terra she was a Camaro fan. Chevy would be disappointed to learn they'd lost her to his old Mustang.

Kevin picked up the phone and punched in the number Terra had given him.

"Hello detective."

"Miss Gallagher I just got a call from..."

"Vince. Yeah I'm not surprised. We ran into each-other earlier as I was comin off mi shift at the station."

"He wants a meet."

"It's ta be expected. Can ya meet now?"

"Yeah I'm at the end of shift anyway."

"Tell im ta be at the Trade Winds in ten minutes."

"Who is he?"

"Old friend."

"I'll pass on the message."

"Thanks detective."

Kevin hung up the phone and called Vince back. He passed on the meet and location before he left.

Terra set down her drink and sighed; it seemed tonight's hunt was off. Between Vince's unexpected visit and the meet at the bar; Jessica's unwanted friend was likely to walk away. "Oh well, another night then," she muttered. Reaching in her purse she pulled out a pack of blacks and put them down on the table.

"I thought you quit?"

"I did. I keep a pack with mi ta maintain the illusion I smoke; it's a cover thing. I said ten minutes Vince, you're early."

"Yeah. Thought I'd get a lay of the land before your detective gets here. How is it you have a cop for a friend? As I recall you tend to shoot cops on principle."

"Things change."

"I guess."

"Are ya goin ta have a seat or do ya intend ta intimidate mi with your shadow loomin over mi all night?"

"I'll sit when he gets here."

"Cute."

"You're driving my car."

"No, I'm drivin a vehicle that draws attention. It's sleek, sexy, classy, and a little sassy but understated. It says look at mi without being overly dramatic. Mi baby is safely stored out of site for later use. The fact that ya used ta drive one had nothin ta do with mi choice." Terra corrected with a hint of temper before picking up her glass and having a sip. Her green eyes moved from Vince to a hint of movement behind him and she smiled.

"Kevin so glad ya could make it," she enthused before standing up and walking past Vince to give the new arrival a hug.

She felt Vince's eyes on them and fought the urge to laugh. It seemed that the hardened operative didn't like how close she was to her friend. It was nice to know she could still push his buttons.

Vince eyed her detective with feigned disinterest; the other man had golden blonde hair and sharp brown eyes. His body was a powerful one, muscled, toned and sun kissed; good looking. He'd been hoping the detective would be an older man and overweight the stereo type build given in bad TV shows, the solid detective but not the lead. As the two embraced Vince felt his playful mood sour. The way they held each other spoke of closeness. Something beyond friendship.

When he'd seen her earlier, he hadn't had any illusions; it had been years since he left her. He'd known there would have been others but it was a little bit disconcerting to be faced with one directly.

"Kevin this is Vince. Vince, meet detective Kevin Hamon."

"Evening," Vince said trying not to let the hostility he felt creep into his tone. He offered his hand to the detective and Kevin took it without hesitation.

"Nice to meet you," Kevin said before he took the empty seat at the table next to Terra. Vince took the seat directly across from her.

"So, Terra said something about a favor?"

"Right. My girl is a DJ at the local station. She's been getting threatening calls, letters, and she's convinced someone's following her. I tailed her a couple days but never saw anyone."

"So, if there is someone following her they're good."

"Right. It made me a little uneasy but nothing to dangerous. Then last week someone took a shot at her."

"Changes the stakes. Moves him from the harmless stalker to threat list."

"I convinced her to take some time off."

"Good move," Vince said with begrudging approval.

"The locals can't find anything. I'm not going to sit by and watch Jessica be terrorized. I tried again to find her stalker myself. But he's real good."

"Nothing?" Vince asked.

"Not even the tell-tale signs of a cigarette butt."

"Damn."

"I thought about a PI but they're expensive. Then I remembered Terra told me if I ever needed anything to call her."

"So, she hopped on a plane and is here trying to draw out Jessica's stalker;" Vince said with a hint of disapproval.

"Yeah." Kevin answered with a laugh.

"How did you two meet?" Vince probed wanting to get a better feel for what that connection was he'd seen earlier.

"I worked a case..."

"That's not your concern Vince. The point here is I'm in town for the reason I said and nothin else," Terra stated interrupting him.

"Okay. Fair enough." Vince relented, if he wanted more he'd either have to get it out of Terra or from the other man when she wasn't around.

"Terra I should get going..." Kevin began.

"Right, tell Jessica I'm handling this. No one will get near her again," Terra said her voice firm.

Kevin nodded and brushed a kiss on her cheek before he got up from the table and left.

Once he was gone Vince spoke again.

"Why'd you retire?"

"It wasn't fun anymore."

"Really, the Terra I knew was so in love with what she did I figured the only way she'd ever leave was if someone took her out."

"Things change Vince."

"I'll say I've never known you to put yourself in someone's cross hairs on purpose."

"The Terra ya knew is dead Vince."

"And Terra-Ann Gallagher."

"She grew up." Terra answered before swallowing the rest of her drink.

"Do you have back-up?"

"No."

"That's a bit careless of you Terra. Never figured you for having a death wish." Vince said with disappointment.

"I can handle this miself Vince."

"Right."

"Oh, you're so smug Mr. Fenton, I always hated that."

"So who is he to you Terra, your cop?"

"Just a friend."

"You told me once you didn't keep friends as they were potential targets."

"That changes when ya retire."

"How did you meet?"

"I told ya it doesn't matter."

"Secrets, really Terra, I thought they weren't your style."

"I learned a few things from mi time with ya," she said bitterly.

"You said before, when I left, I nearly got you killed what does that mean?"

"Kieran didn't take it well."

"What did he do?

"Doesn't matter."

"It does to me."

"I'm not your girl anymore Vince. I never was; I get that. I was an asset. I'm no longer a threat ta ya or of use either. Now be a good little spy and move on. I've got work ta do and you're in mi way," she muttered before rising from the table and walking away.

Vince cursed. He stared at the vacant chair across from him and worry began to stir in his mind. The Terra he remembered wasn't the type to walk away from a fight and she'd done it twice that night. Things did change; he couldn't argue with that but he also knew they didn't change that much. Pulling out his phone Vince punched in the number for one of his contacts.

As the phone rang he blinked realizing she'd not paid for her drink and shook his head. Some things never changed he muttered, as he recalled how with each meet they'd had before, she'd left him to pay her bill. Being stuck with the check now was comforting, as it was familiar.

"Vince."

"Yeah, look I need a favor."

"You got some nerve man calling me at this hour, after getting me shot, for a favor."

"I'm sorry for the hour Jake but keep in mind that bullet kept you out of a mexically prison."

"Right and that's the only reason why we're still talking; so what is it you want."

"Can you look into what happened to my asset in Belfast after I left?"

"That hot little number with the dark hair and bewitching green eyes? What was her name?"

"Terra."

"It'll be my pleasure man. Always wanted..."

"Just research Jake." Vince muttered trying to keep his temper in check. The last thing he wanted right now was to hear about Jake's sex crazed fantasies about Terra when he was paying for her drinks.

"Right... When I've got it you want a location?"

"No just the Intel."

"All right but you'll owe me one Vince."

"Fair enough." Vince answered before he broke the connection. Vince picked up the half-finished shot of whisky she'd left in her rush and threw it back. It burned as it went down and he coughed a little. He hated the stuff but the rim of the glass still tasted like her and despite what he told her all those years before; Terra had meant something to him. Enough so that he was willing to stomach the stuff for that small taste of her wicked mouth.

As Vince set down the shot glass he wondered not for the first time if she left the unfinished drink to punish him. He knew her well enough to know she hated the stuff.

Putting money on the table, he got to his feet; best to move on. Lingering here would only lead to trouble. Picking up his cell phone, Vince punched in the number for his second and waited as the phone rang.

"Vince are you secure?"

"Yes. I've lost my tale and am in the clear. We'll reschedule the mission for tomorrow night. "

"Roger that sir. We'll be at rendezvous point at 1800."

"Good." Vince answered before he ended the call. Satisfied that the job was back on track Vince set down his phone and headed back to the hotel.

Terra pulled the Mustang; Vince claimed was like his; into the garage of the loft she was renting for her cover. She grabbed her things out of the passenger seat and stormed inside.

"Damn him," she'd been in a great mood until he started poking around in her business. She managed to keep Kevin from answering Vince's questions but she knew the man and he'd not let the matter go. Her good mood had fallen flat with the innocent question. How had she met Kevin? It was a simple question and she figured a bit of jealousy drove it but no other question had been more dangerous.

Terra had no intention of telling the annoying spy about what happened after he left. He'd given up the right to know the moment he walked out the door. Terra snarled at the fact she'd run from a fight twice in the same night. She hated running and Vince knew it. He'd pay for making her do so, she vowed, just as soon as this thing with Jessica was cleared up.

As she walked into the main floor space of the two story loft the house phone rang. Terra crossed the floor to where it sat on the kitchen counter and picked up the receiver. "Hello."

Half of her expected to find Vince on the other end. When she got no reply she cursed. Maybe she hadn't lost the stalker's interest after all.

"Hello, is anyone there?"

Her response this time was heavy breathing on the other end.

"Who is this?" she questioned trying to keep the line open to trace the call.

"Did ya miss mi Terra Anne," a man's voice rumbled over the line.

"Kieran, ya bastard this game is between mi and ya. Ya had no right ta bring Jessica into it."

"No right, her beau sent mi ta jail; the prig. Jessica was a warning. He'll pay for his part in mi troubles just as ya will Terra Anne, I made ya and I'll destroy ya darlin," Kieran vowed before falling silent.

"Not if I get ya first," Terra countered.

"Ya won't but ya can try, Oh and Terra luv wear the green nighty for me. I like it best," he added before disconnecting the call. Terra set the phone back in the cradle as if unfazed. Behind the counter her knees shook. Well, now she was sure of it; she was being watched. She felt the need to turn out the lights but curbed the impulse. When Kevin had told her about the shot she'd wondered if it was Kieran but her Intel marked him as dead. She'd wanted to believe the rumors but a part of her had never accepted it.

Fear clawed in her belly and Terra switched off the lights despite her desire to stand firm. She slipped out a window at the back and ran from the loft to the one place she knew was safe.

Vince laid in his bed in that place between sleep and awake. His rest disturbed by the sound of the door clicking shut. He heard soft foot falls on the carpeted floor as he wrapped his hand around the handle of his gun but he didn't stir. He felt the buzz in the air that came with knowing you were being watched and waited for his uninvited guest to make their next move. More foot falls followed by the sound of the fridge opening and closing. A soft curse with a familiar Irish lilt.

His guest turned from the fridge to look at him once more. Green eyes studied him with question before deft hands opened the pilfered liquor and swallowed half of it down. A louder curse followed a light coughing fit at the effect of the whisky he'd left untouched.

Vince felt her gaze settle on him once more and he decided he'd had enough waiting.

"Are you going to stare at me all night Terra or are you going to come to bed?" he asked with a hint of irritation.

"Cocky bastard. While I appreciate the invitation that's not why I'm here Mr. Fenton."

Vince winced at her use of his last name, knowing it was a sign of trouble ahead. He moved to sit up and cursed recalling he wasn't wearing anything.

"I guess your refusal ta get up means ya still prefer ta sleep in the nude Mr. Fenton," she stated amused by his discomfort as she moved closer to his bed.

"I thought you said you weren't here about the bed Terra?"

"I'm not."

"Then why are you here Terra? As I know, it wasn't for my whisky." He muttered changing the subject.

"Did ya leave it then ta get back at mi for the shot earlier? Ya know you didn't have ta drink it."

"I know it, but I wanted to."

"Why?" Terra asked with shock. She knew he hated the stuff.

"Why are you here?" he countered refusing to answer.

"I needed ta get out of mi place for a while."

"The stalker?" Vince asked all hint of teasing evaporated.

"Aye."

"I heard a rumor once that the only time an assassin comes out of retirement is to kill their teacher is that true?" Vince asked

"I don't know." She admitted.

"Is it Kieran you're hunting?"

She blinked at the question; stunned he'd figured it out so quickly. "Why would ya ask that?"

"If you're not here for my bed it means you're here for help. I know when I left, you were the best in your field; second only to your teacher. If you need help it's because you can't handle who's coming after you. I doubt retirement has dulled your skills that much."

"It is Kieran," she admitted.

"What happened between you two after I left Terra? You loved him as if he were your own father?"

"Things change."

"You won't tell me, you're going to make me read it in some report," he asked with disbelief.

"I wish ya'd leave it alone Mr. Fenton," she muttered before she threw back the rest of the bottle. He watched those green eyes of hers widen and her face contorted at the taste of it before she coughed a second time. "Damn that stuff is foul."

"Then why'd you drink it?"

"I wanted ta," she answered echoing his earlier reply.

"Come on Terra, talk to me," Vince entreated.

"Not tonight Vince, I'm sorry, I shouldn't have come here. If he followed mi I may have put ya in danger. I best go."

"Why did you come?"

"Despite what happened between us I always felt safe with ya, Vince." She answered before she turned to go.

"You're sure it's him?"

"Yes." She replied before she reached for the door.

"For what it's worth, I'm sorry I left without a word," Vince said uttering words he'd wanted to say for years. She paused in her departure at his words and sighed.

"I'm sorry I postponed your opp. Finish it Vince and move on. I'll be fine." She assured him. With her peace made Terra left as quietly as she'd come in.

Vince lay back in his bed and closed his eyes. He laughed at his own discomfort caused by being in her presence. Terra Anne Gallagher, she'd always been able to get to him. Vince groaned with frustration at her abrupt departure. He'd wanted her to stay, expected it even.

Hell part of him had figured on her dropping in. It was why he'd had the vodka before bed and elected to sleep without clothes. When they'd been together in Belfast it had been part of their routine. She'd on more than one occasion broken into his place and climbed into his bed unannounced; that was just her way. The Terra he'd known then didn't hesitate or hide. She followed her impulses without shame. That she'd held back tonight troubled him; it wasn't like her. He cursed as he wondered just what that report he'd requested would hold and why she was so keen to keep him from it.

Vince drew a breath to calm himself and growled as her scent assaulted his senses. Terra wasn't one for heavy perfumes or fruity fragrances, no the smell that enticed him now was subtle and uniquely hers. Though she was gone her presence sill lingered to torment him.

He could go after her he realized but understood that to do so was a risk he didn't dare take at least not until his work there in Kauai was done.

Terra slipped back in the loft she was renting and flipped on the lights. She moved through the main room without any hint of fear. The blinds were open allowing anyone to peer in as she moved about. If Kieran was out there, her every move was there for his viewing pleasure. The notion made her skin crawl but she knew the game and if she was going to draw him out she had to make him want to come in.

Stepping into the sleeping area of the loft she slipped behind the screen that separated the public portion of the loft from her private space. She crossed to her dresser and felt her heart stop as she found her green night gown laid out on the bed. So he'd been inside after she left, that proved Jessica's fears founded. She'd claimed her stalker had invaded her home.

Terra ignored the gown opting for a pair of black yoga pants and a green tank. She slipped off her jeans and pulled on the pants before pulling off her pink kami. She un-hooked her bra and reached for the green tank only to have it handed to her.

"I asked you to where the nightie," Kieran's voice muttered with disappointment.

Terra pulled the tank top in place careful to keep her back to him. "Ya don't get to dress mi anymore Kieran as I am no longer in your employ."

"A right shame that is Terra. Ya were mi best pupil," he whispered as he set his hands on her shoulders.

Terra shrugged out of his grip. "What do ya want Kieran?"

"I've come ta offer a truce Terra mi darlin. Come back ta work for mi and all will be forgiven." he answered as he brushed his fingers along her cheek.

"If I refuse?" She asked turning away from his touch.

Kieran grabbed her by the elbow and turned her so they were face to face. "Ya don't want ta be doin that luv."

Terra pulled free of his grasp. "Answer the question."

"Well, then I'm afraid I'll have ta kill ya." Kieran turned her head to the side and brushed his fingers over her jugular as if slitting her throat as he spoke. When he'd delivered the threat his fingers slid down her neck across her collar bone. "I made ya and it's mi right ta break ya; if ya turn on mi."

Terra stepped away from him, her green eyes held contempt. "I see."

"I'll give ya forty-eight hours ta consider the offer."

"What about Kevin and Jessica?" She asked as she crossed her arms over her chest.

"Your cop and his lass will be given the same reprieve, after that all bets are off." Kieran stated as he moved in the direction of the door.

Terra nodded her understanding as a sense of relief filled her at his departure.

"Terra mi dear there is one more thing," he stated as he turned back to face her once more.

"What?" she asked; eyeing him with mistrust.

"I saw ya earlier with your Mr. Fenton." He snapped and was across the room at her side in two strides. "I don't want ta see him around again luv. I'm sure I needn't remind ya what happened the last time he left ya."

Terra flinched as Kieran lifted his hand as if to strike her. Instead he took hold of her chin and tilted her head so their eyes met. "You're mine Terra Anne ya remember that," he murmured before he kissed her. His mouth was hard and demanding, bruising her lips as his hands grabbed hold of her hips and dragged her body against his; pressing his aroused flesh against her.

She wanted to scream at his closeness but she held it in, not giving him anything more than he took. Her body was silent, giving no hint of her discomfort. A lone tear that escaped from her treacherous eye was the only sign of her emotions.

Kieran drew back from her and seeing her tear he wiped it away with the pad of his thumb before tasting it. "Such a strong lass ya are Terra. Ya make mi right proud. Forty-eight hours." he whispered before he brushed a kiss on her brow and left.

Once he was gone Terra sank to the floor; her whole body shaking as she fought back tears. "You'll pay for that Kieran," she vowed when her voice returned. The clock ticking she picked up her phone and punched in Kevin's number.

"Hello."

"Kevin."

"Terra?"

"Yeah, ya remember that discussion we had some time ago."

"About my needing to disappear?"

"Yeah. I'm afraid it's time. Take your lass and go."

"Why? What's happened?"

"Kieran's back. He's the one who is stalking Jessica."

"Damn it. What about you; are you okay?"

"I'll be fine Kevin."

"Shouldn't you be getting out of here?"

"No, I'm goin ta finish this," she answered before she hung up.

Setting her phone down, she crossed to the fridge and pulled out a bottle of vodka. She twisted off the cap and took a swig. She hoped for Vince's sake he did as she told him; finished his job and got out of Kauai.

2 TUESDAY

Vince sat with his team hidden securely inside their appointed safe house; the mission had run like clock-work. There had been no hint of intrusion from the outside and no exposure. The teams cover was intact and the job was done. In a matter of hours he'd be on a plane bound for his next destination and safely out of Kauai. He should have been relieved but instead he was moody and restless.

His eyes shifted from his second in command, a Nordic goddess with a golden tan thanks to three months of the Hawaiian sun, who was in the process of going over their debrief to the alarm clock radio behind her. He noted it was nearly eight and felt his fingers begin to itch. She'd be on at any moment now. Kauai's new Lady of the Night. Terra Anne Gallagher. Unbidden his eyes fell shut at the thought of her.

He pictured her sitting behind the mike, those wicked lips painted a bright red that demanded anyone who saw them pay attention. Thick and full, they were the kind of lips men dreamed about, delectable and dangerous DSL's. He pictured those tempting lips parting and could hear her smoky voice with the Irish lilt pouring out over the airwaves like a siren's song teasing him with the promise of things to come. Vince felt his blood stir with a hunger he'd thought long gone and bit the inside of his cheek to hold back the instinctual groan in response to the fantasy building in his mind.

"Vince, are you listening?" the blonde asked him; derailing his dangerous train of thought.

Vince's eyes popped open instantly. Her interruption as effective as a cold shower, dousing a fire he'd not realized still burned inside him. "Sorry." he muttered half embarrassed to be caught daydreaming and half annoyed to have been interrupted.

"Man, what is with you tonight?" his second asked with irritation to learn he'd lost track of the debrief; it wasn't like him.

"He seems distracted," one of the other members of the team commented.

"Perhaps it has to do with his visitor," the blonde quipped a hint of temper in her tone.

"What visitor?" Vince asked as his full attention settled once more on his second.

"Why don't you tell me?" she asked, her tone had grown harsh now; he noted. The goddess shoved a photo at him in temper. "Who is she?"

Vince blinked as he looked at the 8x10 of Terra as she left his room. Was that fear in her eyes? Vince glared at the photo; rather than the woman who set it in front of him. He hated to be watched and his superiors knew it. "What is this?" he demanded a hint of his temper tinged his voice.

"You said last night you were compromised. I kept watch to see if anyone was watching you?" She explained.

"I told you I'd handle it." Vince muttered. She'd overstepped her bounds and, damn it, if HQ got a hold of that photo he'd have a hell of a lot of explaining to do. The thought of it made him all the more agitated. What did he have to do to prove to them he was not a liability?

"Who is she?" the blonde questioned a second time.

"She's no one," he answered without missing a beat. The lie rolled off his tongue as easily as any other but it sounded strained even to his own ear. He was aware of the fact that the words should be truth. Terra had been an asset. There shouldn't be any lingering feelings for her and yet...

"Right. And I'm just a school teacher. So, is she the reason I can't get past your guard Vince?"

"What?" He asked, startled by the question. He hadn't realized she'd been trying to.

"For a man trained to observe behavior you can be real dense. I've been trying to get past your work persona and into your real life Vince. But you won't give an inch, you keep shutting me out. I want to know is she the reason."

"Why would you ask that?"

"I was told once by one of your fellow operatives that I was wasting my time with you. That I wasn't your type. I figured it was a joke but after seeing you today I've got to wonder if it was a legit warning. Is she the reason?"

"Yes," Vince stated.

"Who is SHE?"

"She's an asset from my work in Belfast. I messed up there. I let her get too close. I ended up blowing my cover as a result. I learned the hard way to keep my distance after her." Vince explained. Terra had been more than an asset to him. His CO had realized it and gotten him clear. He'd never looked back but those green eyes in the photo held fear in their depths and he had to wonder why. What had happened to her after he left and who was this stranger with her face looking back at him because the Terra he knew was gone.

"An Asset. I see and does Snow White have a name?"

"It's one you needn't concern yourself about," Vince answered.

"I think an old asset turning up is something to worry about. I think HQ would agree with me."

"We're out of here in a few hours no need to drag them into this."

"If there's no need then you can answer my question. Who is she?"

Vince cursed not liking being squeezed but knowing if he didn't answer things would only get worse. "Her name is Terra she was a member of the IRA. She was one of their best assassins."

"How did you know she was here?"

"I heard her voice on the radio last night."

"That's why you aborted the mission."

"Yes I thought for sure she was coming after me."

"Is she?"

"No. I met with her and she informed me she is retired. She's here helping a friend."

"If she's not after you then why have I got a picture of her coming out of your hotel room?"

"Terra is a bit unusual in her social visits. She dropped by to pass on some Intel and then left."

"Pass on Intel right," one of the guys laughed.

"Did she mention her friend's name?"

"Yes. He's a local cop I met with him last night it seems his girl has a problem with a stalker and Terra owed him a favor."

"I see."

Vince frustrated, turned on the radio and tuned in the station. He felt a jolt as that sexy voice purred out of the speaker.

"Good evening Kauai and Aloha, from your Lady of the Night as you heard last night I'm filling in for Jessica your own Queen of Cats. It's eight o-clock and Prince Charming is out there somewhere but for now I've kicked off my dancing shoes, my feet are up and I'm going to play the tunes to keep you happy until the witching hour. But first let's start the night off with a song for the city. This one is from me to a special someone out there, I hope you like it."

Vince groaned as the familiar intro to the Police's "I'll be Watching You," played. Did she have a damn death wish? "That was what I heard last night before I aborted mission."

"I don't get it," one of the others muttered.

"The song last night?'

"One way or Another," Vince muttered.

"She was taunting a stalker?" The goddess questioned with disbelief.

"Yes, but I took it as a warning..."

"You thought the message was for you," the one man said with a laugh.

"Man talk about ego," the other muttered.

"Did she say anything about who the stalker might be?"

"No." Vince lied this time without any hint of his deception.

"But you're worried," his second stated.

"A little," Vince admitted.

"Then Terra is more to you than an asset. She's pretty if you go for that sort of thing," the goddess muttered before she picked up the photo and tore it up assuring him HQ would hear nothing about it from her.

Terra sat in the booth listening to the last song set wind down. As she switched on her mike she smiled. She had to admit this was fun.

"Hello caller you're on the air," she whispered.

"Hello, Terra how are ya doin tonight?"

Terra froze; recognizing the man's voice but didn't let it faze her.

"I'm doing pretty well."

"I'm glad ta hear that. Ya had mi worried last night. I wasn't sure ya'd keep it together," The voice on the other end said with an eerie calm.

"You scared mi a little," Terra admitted a bit of her natural accent slipping out as the hair on the back of her neck stood on end. It was him. Kieran had called her at the station proving he was watching her every move. The truth of it made her stomach knot with fear.

"I'm sorry luv, but I needed ta make myself clear. Ya had a busy night what with your time at the station and then the meet at the bar. Going back out ta meet with your Mr. Fenton and then our chat. You must be tired."

"Yes, I had a very busy night," Terra murmured as a chill ran through her body he was watching her every move. What else did he know about her that he shouldn't?

"Have ya considered mi offer?" He asked.

"I'm still thinking about it," Terra answered.

"Twenty four hours Terra Anne. Don't make mi wait too long." Kieran muttered before he hung up.

"You heard it here folks, Prince Charming has asked me to his palace for the ball and I've got until the witching hour tomorrow to accept. But in the mean time I'll be here taking your requests. Here's a special one for you Kauai I hope you like it," She murmured before she cued up Bonnie Tyler's "I need a Hero".

Once the song was playing she switched off her mike and drew a breath; she'd thought she could handle Kieran, she'd figured enough time had passed that the fear she'd once known every day would have subsided; she'd been wrong.

Vince cursed as the new song played; he'd heard the call. His eyes flicked over to his second and he waited for a comment.

"Vince it seems to me your asset needs you."

Vince nodded.

"What about headquarters," one of the others asked.

"Vince decided to stay on the island for his past due leave," the goddess answered.

"Thank you."

"Get going."

Vince rose from his seat and made his way from the safe house to his X-Runner; getting in the truck he drove across town back to the station. He pulled up out font and killing the engine he looked around for any signs of Kieran but found none. He knew the other man was out there and was cautious as he approached the station.

As he walked in the building he read the signs indicating the studio location and walked past the receptionist at the front desk without a word. Alarmed she rose from her seat to give chase.

"Sir, you can't go back there," the receptionist called as she ran after him. He ignored her. His brown eyes searching for any sign of Terra; fear gripping him. "Sir, Stop. Security!" The woman shouted as he reached the booth.

"Hello, Kauai, this is your 'Lady of the Night' again and I just want to assure all of you I'm still here and will be until the final strike of the clock at midnight. I've kicked off my glass slippers and am ready to dance the night away, so keep sending your requests and we'll heat up the night. Thank you, for all your calls and now let's hear a tune by Jennifer Paige."

Vince watched as she switched off her mike and pressed a button to start the music "Crush". Damn her; was she trying to piss him off. Part of him wanted to shake some sense into her, since she seemed unfazed by the threat. Then there was the other half of him that had dreamt about that haunting voice last-night and that side of him was thinking of ways to get her attention. Not liking one bit being ignored when she'd called for his aid.

At the moment he saw himself crossing to her side; turning her towards him and capturing her bewitching mouth with his own as he backed her against a wall.

Vince blinked this wasn't the time to get distracted, he had to stay focused; her life was at stake.

"Are you crazy or just stupid?" he snapped.

"Neither, I have work ta do go away."

"Go away, you called me here," Vince said his temper flaring.

"I panicked Vince. Ya shouldn't be here. If he sees ya..."

"Oh no you don't. You called, I'm here and you're going to start explaining what he was talking about."

"Not now Mr. Fenton I have ta work." She said brushing him off.

"You have work, he threatened you on the air and made it sound like he paid you a visit last night," Vince began with rage.

"I'm not goin ta let Kieran get ta mi Vince that's what he wants," Terra said sharply.

"Damn it, Terra. Don't play with this guy he's dangerous."

"Ya think I don't know that?"

"You called for my help and you got it. From now on you're not going to be alone. When you go out for anything I'm going with you."

"Damn ya Vince don't do this. I told ya last night ta move on and I meant it. I won't be responsible for his killin ya. Which is exactly what will happen if he finds ya here. Go. I can take care of miself."

"Let him try I'll welcome the chance to get my hands on that son of a bitch."

"He's a trained assassin Vince, ya won't get your hands on him. Ya won't even see him comin. Do us both a favor and forget I called for aid. Get on the next plane out of Kauai and don't look back."

"Sorry princess, you're stuck with me. Now you have a choice, I can stay at your place or you can stay with me tonight; either way I know you're protected." Vince said coolly before stepping out of the booth ending the discussion.

He saw her green eyes spark with challenge as he turned but at that same moment security turned up with the receptionist. "There he is, I want him arrested…"

"Marge, it's okay, he's a friend. He just came in ta make sure I was okay," Terra said quickly before ducking back into the booth this conversation would have to wait until later.

"Oh, okay. I'm sorry sir."

"Don't be, I'm glad to see someone is on guard. I'm sorry if I frightened you," Vince said calmly. "I'll be making sure Terra gets home safely tonight."

"Oh, good, I was afraid I was going to have to call for a police escort."

"No, need. I'll see to her," Vince assured her before taking a seat outside the booth. It was going to be a long night.

Vince groaned as the last ten minutes until midnight ticked down. The past few hours had been torture. Terra had ignored him completely since his arrival and her clear dismissal of him was slowly driving him crazy. He'd forgotten how difficult she could be. She didn't want him there and her refusal to acknowledge his presence was her way of showing it. As far a she was concerned the argument they'd started was over and he was leaving. "The hell I am," he muttered to himself.

She'd called him and whether she liked it or not he was staying, the where was up to her but if he had his way it would be at his place. Given her mood he figured he wouldn't get his way and sighed. He didn't care. Terra wasn't getting hers either. The second she was off the air for the night they were finishing their discussion. He was not going to be ignored.

"Good evening, Kauai this is your personal, Lady of the Night. We're nearing the witching hour ladies and gents. I'm with you for another five and then unless I hit the door I'll be turning into a pumpkin. But there's enough time tonight for one last request."

Vince held his cell phone next to his ear and listened to it ring.

"Hello, Caller you're on the air what can I get for you tonight?"

"Yeah, can you play a song for me?" Vince asked.

"Sure, anything in particular?" Terra asked. He noted the question in her voice as she became aware of whom the voice on the other end belonged to.

"Yeah, *Two Steps Behind; by Def Leopard,* send it out to Kauai's Lady of the Night," Vince said before he hung up.

He watched with satisfaction as Terra's head lifted and her bewitching eyes lit with temper as she glared at him. He smiled. She wasn't ignoring him anymore. As soon as the song was cued up she came out of the booth.

"Have ya gone mad? Ya just marked yourself for death," she snapped.

"It got you out here didn't it?" he said amused.

"Oh, ya don't play fair Mr. Fenton."

"So, where are we staying tonight?"

"I'll be goin home and I suggest ya go back to that hotel of yours; pack your things and hop the first flight out of town."

"I told you that's not going to happen."

"You're bein rather careless with your life Vince."

"I walked away once Terra, I won't do it again."

"What makes ya think ya got the right ta interfere in mi life Mr. Fenton?"

"Because it was you that dropped in on me unannounced in the middle of the night." he said getting to his feet.

"Old habit," she said dismissively taking a step back.

"You sent the S.O.S." He argued taking a step toward her.

"I panicked." she admitted.

"You need my help." He muttered as he closed the distance between them. "You want me here Terra," he added as he grabbed her by the arm drawing her against him so that they stood eye to eye. "You're just too stubborn to admit it and we both know it." He lowered his head to capture her lips and she turned away.

"That's enough Vince." She said drawing back, fear beginning to creep in on her. Vince drew back shocked by her withdrawal; Terra had never rebuffed his advance; she'd always welcomed it, now she looked almost spooked. He wondered why but said nothing; giving her the space she silently demanded.

"If ya have any notions about pickin up where we left off ya can forget em," Terra said moving away from him.

Vince nodded. "Why?"

"I won't get burned for ya again," she muttered.

"Burned? What happened after I left?"

"I told ya it was none of your concern." Terra snapped.

"How bad is it going to be when I get that report?" Vince asked with concern.

"Forget the report Vince, please," she requested.

"Did he hurt ya?"

Terra laughed at the question, a bitter cold laugh that chilled his blood. "Of course he hurt mi. Ya left and turned out ta be a spy. I brought ya into the midst of his circle. I was punished for bringin ya in. Damned as a traitor. It was only because I was his protégée that I'm still alive."

"Why is he back then?"

"I don't know," she muttered with irritation before she headed for the door.

"Terra," he called to stop her. Afraid she really was going to shut him out completely.

Terra stopped mid stride and sighed. "Are ya comin or not, Mr. Fenton?" she questioned before starting off again. Vince didn't hesitate he was at her side in a few strides and escorting her out of the building. He walked her to her car and then moved back to his truck. When she pulled out, he followed her at a distance watching for Kieran but he didn't see anything. Either the man had already left or he was lying in wait at her home.

As he trailed after her, Kieran's comment about his visit with her had him wondering again what her former handler had meant. As he drove on he pulled out his cell phone and punched in Jake's number.

"Hello?"

"Jake how is the research coming?"

"Slow. Someone went to a lot of trouble to bury that Intel."

"How long?"

"Two or three days at least."

"Get it to me before Friday and I'll throw in a bonus," Vince offered.

"Why the rush?"

"Something's going on here and I haven't got the whole picture yet; until I do I can't do my job effectively."

"She's holding out on you, that's not like Terra."

"I know and that's the problem. She's changed drastically. Something's off. I just don't know what or why?"

"I'll see if I can shed some light on the subject," Jake stated.

"Thanks I owe you one."

"You're welcome but I'm going to hold you to that." Jake teased before he hung up.

Vince put his phone down as he turned on to Terra's drive. He'd reached their destination. It was time to step into the lair of the huntress. As he stepped out of his truck, he realized that once he crossed the threshold into her domain there was no turning back; he'd be a marked man for sure.

Terra turned to look at him, her eyes questioned if he was really going to do this. He said nothing, didn't hesitate. As soon as the door was open he stepped inside gun at the ready. If Kieran was there he was going to get a rude welcome.

Terra flipped on the lights and Vince cursed, every window in the loft was uncovered allowing her stalker to watch her every move making her an easy target.

"Why not just shoot yourself and save him the bullet," Vince grumbled with disgust.

"Do ya think he's at an advantage then Mr. Fenton?" Terra asked with amusement.

"From what I see you might as well have left the door open for him."

"Ya never fully understood the assassin's game did ya Vince?" she said with disappointment.

"I was never fond of thinking of assassination work as a game Terra. That's one game that leads to innocent people dying," Vince stated.

"The art of deterrin a sniper's fire is ta make the gunman think that if he's set up from an easy line that before he can take his shot ya have yours. If ya look you'll find that every line he might take is covered. He can see mi movements but he can't make a move. If he does I have him, or someone will see and I still have him."

"Big gamble for a friend."

"Kevin's more than a friend Vince."

"Meaning?"

"He's family."

"Kieran was family and you're trying to blow his head off."

"Kieran isn't kin anymore he's an oath breaker," Terra hissed.

Vince stared at her stunned. He recalled the term from his days in Belfast. An oath breaker was one marked an outcast by the family they were worse than traitors. He wondered what Kieran had done to earn the label from her when she'd once been closer to him than her own father. "Am I?" he asked unable to keep the question to himself.

"No, don't be ridiculous Mr. Fenton. Ya may be a lot of things but traitor and oath breaker aren't one of them," she said with disbelief at the question as if it was foolishness.

"Was he here last night after you came back?"

"Aye."

"What happened?"

"He asked mi ta come back ta work for im."

"You said he scared you?"

"Got too close. Threatened to cut mi throat," Terra explained.

"Why? If he wants your help, isn't threatening you, like that, counterproductive."

"He didn't want mi gettin mixed up with ya again."

"What are you going to tell him?"

"No. I won't go back to workin for that oath breaker."

"What happened Terra?"

"If ya want ta stay Vince Fenton ya won't ask mi that question again."

Vince nodded his acceptance of the rule; he didn't like it but at least he'd won the first battle; she wasn't going to send him away. He'd get the information, eventually, one way or the other, for now he'd settle for what was given and build upon it.

Terra smiled pleased to have won that piece of the argument she moved through the loft to the closet and pulled out an extra blanket and a pillow. "Hope ya don't mind the couch," she said before moving up the stairs to the second floor behind her security screen where the bed was.

Vince took the blanket and tossed it on the couch. It wasn't quite the home coming he'd been hoping for but at least he'd gotten his foot in the door. It was a start. Vince looked up to the second floor and watched as she stretched stiff limbs and cursed; it was going to be a long night.

3 WEDNESDAY

Vince woke a little after ten as the sunlight streamed in the living room. He blinked, taking in his surroundings as the night before came back to his mind. Glancing upstairs he noted that his hostess wasn't up yet. Sitting up he grunted, the couch had not been kind to his back but he'd live. After stretching stiff joints he got to his feet and began going through the motions of starting his day.

Once refreshed and dressed he moved out into the living room and studied the layout of the house. He was impressed Terra hadn't been exaggerating last night, she had every angle covered. But the fact that Kieran had gotten into the loft without her knowledge didn't sit well with him and he was going to do something about it.

Grabbing his keys; he crossed to the kitchen and scribbled a note for her that he'd stepped out but would be back. He then slipped out the front door. As soon as he emerged from the loft his palms began to sweat and the hair on the back of his neck stood on end. Kieran was out there watching. Vince could feel the cross hairs on him and he smiled. Good he had the other man's attention.

"Come and get me you Irish prick," he muttered in challenge before he slipped behind the wheel of his x-runner and sped off. He felt the heightened sense of danger ease and cursed. He'd hoped he could draw the assassin away from the loft but it seemed Kieran wasn't biting; not yet anyway. Vince considered going back, worried that leaving Terra alone may not be his best move, but he needed a failsafe and he'd have to gamble. The supplies he needed weren't at the loft and taking her with would only ensure that her stalker saw what he was up to.

Figuring Terra could handle herself he drove on. Heading into the city to gather supplies.

Terra was torn from sleep, by the sound of Vince's truck door slamming, with a jolt. She blinked, startled as she slipped out of the bed. She cursed to find he'd left. Last night had been the best night's sleep she'd had in a long time. Knowing Vince was there had helped her to relax. She wondered where he'd gone, without a word. as she pulled on her robe.

Terra moved downstairs into the main room and felt a chill at the feel of the snipers scope focused on her. She waved at her stalker before focusing her own weapon in his direction, reminding him that she could see him as well, before moving into the kitchen.

As she came to the fridge to get herself a bottle of water she spotted the note Vince had left for her.

"Went for supplies be back soon." She shook her head before crumpling the note and tossing it in the trash. "What sort of supplies is that?" she muttered before moving back into the center of the loft. She moved back upstairs and after a swig of her water crawled back into bed; it was still early yet and she wasn't ready to be up. Terra drew a gun from the nightstand and slid it under her pillow before she laid back and closed her eyes. Kieran wasn't going to catch her off guard again.

Vince pulled into a parking space in front of a small privately owned local hardware store. Getting out of the truck he stepped inside and started down the aisles with purpose. He picked up a basket and pulled various items off the shelves as he went. Among them were some copper wire, a soldering iron, batteries, nuts and bolts and the wrenches to go with them. He grabbed a roll of electrical tape and a pair of vice grips before heading to the counter. Vince paid for the items with cash then moved back out to the lot. He tossed the bag in the passenger seat before he pulled out of the lot and moved on to his next stop.

Terra groaned with frustration as she gave up on going back to sleep. She was awake and nothing was going to change that. Annoyed she crawled out of bed for a second time and moved into the master bath. She was careful to keep the light out as she pulled off her sleep clothes and pulled on her exercise gear. While she knew the dark wasn't complete security it at least gave her a bit of privacy so long as Kieran wasn't using a night-vision scope.

She closed her eyes at the thought and tried not to cringe. She hoped he wasn't. Once changed she moved back downstairs and began her morning routine with her workout. As she tumbled and rolled and threw strikes at an invisible enemy she was keenly aware of Kieran's eye fixed upon her. She struggled to remain calm.

"Damn ya Vince where are ya?" she muttered.

Vince set his purchase from the auto parts store behind his seat before pulling out into traffic. He turned the truck in the direction of Terra's loft. With a little luck he'd get back before she even woke and Terra would never know he'd gone, Vince mused. His gaze landed on a small cafe as he sat at a light and he turned into the lot. If she was up a peace offering couldn't hurt, Vince reasoned as he got out of the truck. He made his way up the sidewalk, the smell of fresh cinnamon and bread hit his senses and he smiled.

Yeah Terra would love this gesture, he assured himself as he approached the counter to place his order.

Terra sat on the matted floor her knees pressed to her chest as she drew deep breaths and tried to relax. She'd worked herself harder than usual to burn through her nervous energy. She admitted to herself that she wasn't sure if it was caused by the knowledge Kieran was watching or if it had to do with Vince's having been under her roof. There was a chance too that it was due to the fact the last time he left her a note like that he'd never come back.

Terra was just starting to level out when the front door opened and Vince walked in. Her green eyes took him in; tall and lean with a dark complexion his brown eyes studied her with an intensity that sent a new wave of nervousness in her. As he moved towards her she got to her feet uncomfortable with his towering over her so. While he was not built with the appearance of strength she knew his appearance was deceptive. He was strong enough to snap her in two.

"Where'd ya go?" she asked.

"For a few things. I got breakfast while I was at it," he said as he held out a bag to her. Terra took it and upon opening it the smell of fresh cinnamon and citrus wafted out tempting her nostrils and making her mouth water. "Thank ya," she whispered with delight as she pulled the pastry out. She sank her teeth into the orange glazed cinnamon roll and moaned with pleasure as the sweet hit her taste buds.

Vince grinned amused at her enthusiasm. He stood and watched her as she ate. Seeing her eyes light up with her enjoyment his thoughts drifted to memories of a time when she'd looked much the same, her hair mussed, sweat glistening from her body and that look of bliss in her eyes as they'd made love. Best not go there Vince, he told himself as he drew his eyes away from her. He could feel Kieran watching him. Now wasn't the time to get distracted.

"I need you to draw the drapes."

"What, why? We went over this last night..." Terra began with confusion. Her eyes lifted from her treat to the man who'd given it and she noted a spark of hunger there she'd not seen in a long time. Her mind tensed with alarm even as she felt her body stir in response to him. She dismissed the reaction to circumstances. Part of her had worried he wouldn't come back.

"I know but I want to set up a couple traps to deter Kieran from coming in and they'll be useless if he sees where they are," Vince muttered.

"Traps, Vince that's not..."

"Do you want him coming in and out of here as he pleases because if you do I can leave right now?"

"Of course I don't but traps are dangerous; one wrong step..."

"I can assure you, I'll be careful," Vince offered.

Terra nodded before turning and moving upstairs to shower and change. Vince watched her go unable to look away, the need to follow her was a strong one but he ignored it; turning instead to the task at hand. He drew the drapes and began the work of setting his traps for the trained assassin watching their every move. If Kieran tried to come in unannounced again, he'd be in for an unpleasant experience.

Vince pulled out the various supplies and turned his attention to creating a pressure switch activated fire trap out of the assortment of parts he'd purchased earlier. He was just finishing up the first device when Terra reemerged from the bathroom dressed and ready to face the day ahead.

"You're not goin ta make it smell like harsh cleaners in here are ya?"

"Of course not, we have to be able to live here," Vince stated.

"Good because if it smells like kerosene Kieran will know what you're up ta."

"Have some faith Terra," Vince requested as he folded the area rug near the door back into place concealing the trigger.

"Sorry, I haven't worked with a pro in a while," she confessed.

"Its fine Terra," he assured her as he moved to her side. With the drapes drawn he leaned down and captured her lips with his own. Giving into the need to taste her, if only for a moment.

Terra gasped startled by his advance but gave no protest. Unable to resist him. It had been that way with him from the start. There was something about Vince Fenton that drew her like the moon pulled the sea. It burned in her blood like a drug and left her desperate for more. Reckless with her need to have it. Terra kissed him back; her mouth hard and ruthless in its demand for him. Her arms wrapped around his shoulders, her nails biting into his skin as she drew him closer.

Vince groaned with need as his hands took hold of her firm rear and dragged her to him so that the center of her feminine body was pressed snuggly against his tightening groin. He watched as dark lashes fluttered and green eyes flew open to stare back at him. She blinked as if waking from a trance and shrank back from him.

"No, we can't do that, not again. I won't let ya do this ta mi," she panted with determination as she wiped her lips with the back of her hand, removing his kiss.

Vince eased his grip on her with regret. She was more than ready for him, it showed in her eyes but he'd respect her request for space. "I'm sorry I just..."

"No need, I let miself get lost in memories of the past. I'm sorry I won't let ya hurt mi again Vince," she muttered before she stepped out of the circle of his arms and crossed to the windows. She drew a calming breath as she pulled the shades letting the all seeing eye of Kieran penetrate the room once more. She'd have to be more careful where Vince was concerned. The closer she let him get, the more danger she was putting him in.

"I never meant to hurt you Terra Anne. I was trying to protect you," Vince explained in his defense.

"I know why ya left Vince but it didn't take long for it ta feel like you'd abandoned mi."

"I'd never do that."

"But ya did," she muttered before moving back in the direction of the room, she had several hours before she had to be back at the station yet and with a little luck she'd be able to slip back to sleep now that he was back.

"Terra..." Vince began but she didn't respond she just kept walking. "Terra-Ann please wait."

"I waited five years Vince. I'm not waitin another second for ya." She snapped before she sank down into her bed with her back to him.

Vince cursed as she shut him out. "I shouldn't have kissed her," he muttered to himself; aware he'd moved too fast for her. The fact of it puzzled him, Terra had never been one to wait. She was a shoot first and ask questions later sort of girl. Where sex was concerned she'd had a considerable and demanding appetite. There was a time when she'd been the one to rush; now she hesitated and he worried at it.

Upstairs Terra lay in her bed, eyes closed, but sleep was once again beyond her reach. Her body hummed with desire as images of what had just passed between them played out in her mind. She could still feel Vince's aroused flesh pressed against her and she bit her lip to repress the verbal response to the sensation. Memories of the past began to fill her mind with images of their passion.

Terra opened her eyes to run from the vivid reminders of who they had been to each other. "Damn him, it's not fair how he gets ta mi," she muttered to herself as her flesh heated with the need of his touch. Using the mirror by the bed she gazed downstairs to where she'd left him and found him once more lying on the couch.

She considered going down to him and bringing him back to her bed where she wanted him. From the kiss they'd just shared she knew he would be receptive but she didn't move. She wasn't ready to go there yet. Kieran was watching, but that wasn't the reason for her hesitation she didn't want Vince to see yet what her mentor had done to her. As her thoughts turned to her punishment her body cooled and the images of that night threatened to fill her mind. No, she wasn't ready to admit to Vince what had happened after he left.

Picking up her cell phone she sent a text to her contact in Belfast and bid them buy her a few more days before the Intel Vince was looking for came to light. She then set the alarm on her phone to wake her in time to get ready for the nights show.

Terra rose a little after six and moved downstairs to fix herself a meal. She stopped by the couch and studied Vince with regret and longing. He didn't belong there. She needed to convince him to leave. Kieran had taken a lot of things from her over the years she wasn't going to add Vince's life to that list.

"You always did like to watch me sleep," Vince sighed as he opened his eyes.

"Sorry. I'm fixin a meal and wanted ta know if ya wanted anythin."

"I'll get something on the way to the station," Vince stated.

She nodded before turning away from him for the kitchen.

"What's on your mind Terra? It's not like you to hold stuff back."

"I want ya ta leave Vince."

She watched as he got to his feet; his brown eyes hard and cold with irritation. "I thought we'd been through this I'm not going anywhere without you."

"Vince I can handle Kieran alone. Ya don't belong here anymore."

"You don't mean that Terra Anne and I want to know why you'd say it."

"Ya gave up the right ta know the day ya walked out mi door and mi life."

"Terra," he growled his voice thick with impatience.

She flinched and he blinked, shocked his temper had shaken her. The woman he'd known had never been troubled by it; she'd enjoyed it using the mix of temper and hunger to shred his careful control and unleash the more demanding and possessive side of his nature. Arguments had often ended in intense and rough sex, they'd both thrilled in.

"Talk to me," he requested gently.

"I won't see ya dead Vince, not because of mi."

"You think I can't handle him?" Vince questioned with disbelief.

"I think you're an accomplished agent Mr. Fenton but that doesn't make ya a match for a master assassin. If he decides he wants ya dead, you'll be dead and I won't stand over your grave."

"Kieran won't use a bullet to kill me Terra. His ego won't allow it. When he does come after me it'll be face to face. He'll want to prove he can handle me on my terms. Want to prove he's the better man. When he does I'll have him."

"What if you're wrong?"

"I'm not. So long as I'm here he's watching me; not you. That's how I want it." Vince stated.

"Ya don't have ta shield mi Mr. Fenton."

"Yes, I do. It's what I promised you in Belfast."

"That was long ago Vince, I don't expect ya ta..."

"I never turned my back on that promise," he whispered before he brushed a kiss on her forehead. Terra's eyes fell shut at his closeness and she drew a deep breath as her mind was eased. "Go make your dinner, we'll discuss this later."

Terra nodded before she moved into the kitchen. Vince watched as she prepared her dinner with ease. Aware of his eye on her but at ease and he smiled. There she was; his Terra, nerves of steel nothing touched her. The skittish woman who had been talking to him of late was disconcerting.

Vince watched the domestic scene and chuckled, he never thought he'd see the day when Terra Anne was focused on making a meal instead of plastique or assembling her weapon. As he watched her now he wondered where the riffle was. He'd seen a number of other guns but not the one that marked her profession.

Terra ate her meal in silence aware Kieran had her marked she held her own weapon trained on him and dared him to make a move as soon as he did he'd be done. She felt the moment her mentor's focus moved from her to Vince and shook her head. Despite Vince's assurance that Kieran wouldn't shoot him her stomach clenched with fear. He might shoot just to hurt her she wouldn't put it past him.

When she was done eating the pair left the loft and headed for the station. Vince stopped on the way as he'd said but when she entered the station he was right behind her. He gave a nod to the receptionist from the night before as he walked past to take up a seat once more outside the studio booth.

Terra slid into her chair behind the mike and prepared her material for the night. She chose her song for the night and smiled, she hoped he liked it. With everything set she waited for the last song to wind down before switching on her mike and beginning the show.

"Good evening Kauai and Aloha, from your Lady of the Night. For those of you that have been listening, as you heard Monday, I'm filling in for Jessica, your own Queen of Cats, this week. It's eight o-clock and Prince Charming is out there somewhere but for now I've kicked off my dancing shoes, my feet are up and I'm going to play the tunes to keep you happy until the witching hour. But first let's start the night off with a song for the city. This one is from me to a special someone out there I hope you like it."

As she switched off the mike having cued up the song she heard Vince chuckle as he muttered, *"The Touch*, Stan Bush, cute," and shook her head. It was strange to be communicating with him over the airwaves but he seemed to be enjoying it as much as she was as the line began to ring she wondered if he'd call her again.

It was a little after nine when she heard his familiar voice on the line.

"Aloha caller you're on the air."

"Hello could you play a song for me?"

"What can I get for you?'

"Chris Daughtry's "Crashed into You", send it out to The Lady of the Night from her someone special," he requested before hanging up the phone.

Terra cued up the song and laughed before poking her head out of the booth. "You're goin ta get mi in trouble," she said with a laugh.

"When are you not in trouble," he teased.

"I've got a job ta do here. I don't need ya distractin mi."

"Would you prefer I dedicate them to Terra?"

"That would be better," she admitted.

"All right then."

Terra turned and moved back into the booth. She wondered when Kieran would call as the song wound down and found she didn't have to wait long. She took several requests off the air but when it was time to go live and she flipped over she found him waiting on the other end.

"Aloha caller what can I do for you tonight?"

"Hello Terra mi dear I've been enjoyin the show but you'd be wise ta tell your Mr. Fenton to stop callin in. I'm not fond of listenin ta ya talk ta im."

"Hello Prince Charming, and how are you tonight?"

"I'm well Terra, mi sweet it's mighty kind of ya ta ask."

"What can I get you tonight Prince Charming?"

"Time's almost up. Have ya made up your mind?"

"Yeah, I'm not interested."

"A shame. But I can't say I'm surprised really."

"Why is that?"

"Because ya continue ta disappoint mi luv."

"Meaning.

Ya can't begin ta imagine mi disappointment at seein mi 'Lady of the Night' in the company of another man. If I thought for a moment your Mr. Fenton had any real designs on making ya his, I'd snap im in two. Are ya still in love with im Terra-Ann?" Kieran questioned his voice hinting at barely contained anger.

Terra's heart froze with fear at the threat toward Vince, for a moment she couldn't speak until she reminded herself he was a trained agent. He could more than handle himself. "He's just a friend," she replied easily even though it seemed harder to breathe.

"I'm glad ta hear that, though I have mi doubts. He seemed awful quick in ta play your rescuer. Does he think that he can protect ya then?"

"What do you mean?" Terra asked feigning ignorance.

"Ya know what I mean, Terra Anne. I see im in there sittin outside the booth watchin. He can't keep mi from ya. You're mine, Terra. I made ya and if ya defy mi I will destroy ya. I will come for ya mi lady, when the time is right. You'll see, we'll be together mi luv, as we were meant ta be," the voice said sweetly before the phone went dead.

Terra switched off her mike and cued up a song as she fought the impulse to tear off her headphones and run. Her skin crawled with disgust as another chill ran through her. She felt the need to be sick and shoved it violently away as the phones erupted with noise. Going wild with calls no doubt in response to the live call and her abrupt shift to music without a word. People listening who were worried about her, but she couldn't bring herself to respond just yet.

She wanted to scream but didn't. She wasn't willing to allow the display of fear. She felt violated but wasn't ready to deal with anything she felt just yet. He was watching and she wouldn't give him the satisfaction. Pulling herself together she picked up the phone to answer it getting back to work.

Vince having heard enough rose from his seat and stepped in the booth. As he entered he heard Terra assure a caller she was fine and then take their request. She glanced over at him for a moment acknowledging his presence before returning to the phones.

"You okay?' he questioned.

Terra nodded and he moved back out into the hall. He'd not seen anyone enter but her abrupt switch from broadcast to music had shaken him. Part of him had been convinced he'd step in the booth and find it empty Kieran having taken her. The notion was ridiculous but the fear had gnawed at him. When his gaze fell upon her and he'd heard that seductive voice, his dread had subsided. She was still there.

Terra switched on her mike sending her smoky voice once more over the airwaves.

"Aloha Kauai, I just wanted to ease your fears the Prince hasn't dragged me off to the ball, I'm still here. My glass slippers are off and my feet are up. We've still got a few hours until the witching hour when I change from siren to mouse so give me a call and I'll keep playing the songs you want to heat up your night. This one goes out to Jessica from Kevin I hope you like it." *(Amazed by LoneStar)*

When midnight arrived Terra took off her head phones and stepped out of the booth. She started down the hall in the direction of the exit and Vince grabbed her by the arm dragging her into the ladies room, they were going to talk now without Kieran watching.

"How the hell did he know I was outside the booth there's no window to see in?" Vince said with disbelief.

"Could be he's tapped into the security feed," Terra answered.

"I'll look into it."

"Vince I wish you'd..."

"I'm not leaving Terra Anne so save your breath. He said he'd break me in two; I'd like him to try it. We both know I can take him."

"What if he decides ta shoot instead just ta hurt mi?"

"He won't and he won't get close enough to hurt you again either," Vince assured her before he kissed her.

Terra turned away reluctantly. "I'm not ready for ya ta get that close again Mr. Fenton I don't know if I ever will be," she said with regret.

"I'm sorry I hurt you Terra it was never my intent," he whispered.

"I know, but ya did and I'm not lookin ta get hurt again. Can we go, I'm tired," she said feeling more worn out than she could ever remember.

Vince nodded. The pair slipped from the bathroom into the main hall. Terra got in her car and started for the loft aware of Vince following at a distance, as she turned onto her street the phone strapped to her hip vibrated. Signaling an incoming text. Unclipping the phone she pressed the button to view it.

"If ya let him touch ya again lass I'll make ya suffer for it. Leave the sky light open for mi we need ta talk Terra Anne."

Terra cursed as she pulled into her drive. How did he plan on pulling that off with Vince staying under her roof she wondered as she deleted the text? As she made her way to the door she was careful to keep distance between her and Vince. She had no interest in dealing with the consequences Kieran would bring down on her if she failed to do as he said. Once inside she moved upstairs and prepared for bed behind the cover of her security screen she unlatched the skyline lock as instructed before sinking down on the bed.

She watched as Vince stretched out on the couch and with her gun still tucked under the pillow waited for Kieran to show.

4 Thursday

It was a little after 3am when Terra became aware she was no longer alone on the second floor. She didn't see him but she could feel Kieran's presence around her watching her at a distance waiting. She rolled over in her bed and gun raised pointed into the darkness.

"Ya don't need that Terra mi luv,'" he whispered from the shadows.

"I disagree ya threaten mi and think I won't protect miself after last time."

"Fair enough, though I'd hoped our next meetin would have been in private," he said with irritation.

"What makes ya think ya have the right ta be here at all?"

"I made ya Terra Anne took ya from a helpless unnoticed chit and turned ya into a strikin confident woman with the skills ta protect herself against any threat."

"I left that life Kieran."

"Ya had no right ta Terra darlin ya were mine."

"I was never yours Kieran. I was with Mr. Fenton."

"Aye, I know but ya had no call ta be with him. Ya were always mine. I was just waitin for the right time ta claim ya."

"Ya were with your pretty Miss Walsh did ya think I was the kind of girl ta share ya?"

"No I didn't. I was done with Pamela ya know that."

"I never saw ya that way Kieran. Ya were mi da not mi luv."

"With time you'll learn ta love mi," he assured her.

"I'll never be yours Kieran, not after what ya did."

"We'll see," Kieran answered before he stepped out of the shadows to stand at her side. He twisted her arm taking her gun with an ease born from years of experience and flipped the safety back on. "Ah now this takes mi back, a simple black nine millimeter berretta. The first one I ever gave ya. Did ya think ya could shoot mi with it

Terra?" he asked amused. He used her arm to draw her against him and drew in the smell of her.

"Such a lovely scent ya have lass I've been trying ta find the soap for miself but I'm not havin much luck perhaps I'll slip into the bath before I go and take it," he taunted before he lowered his head to kiss her. She bit his lip in defense against his advance and he hit her before licking the blood from his skin. "Ya always were a feisty one Terra Anne. Do ya think drawin mi blood will stop mi from takin back what's mine?" he asked amused as he ran the barrel of the gun against her ivory skin in a sick caress. It ran down from her temple along her cheek sliding against her neck and into the cleavage left by her night clothes.

"Don't" she hissed in warning. "All I have ta do is scream."

Kieran flipped off the safety and wrapped his finger around the trigger. "I'll squeeze long before ya get the chance," he countered before he kissed her once more. His lips were cruel and demanding bruising hers as he reclaimed them as his alone. When he was satisfied that he'd removed any lingering touch from her Mr. Fenton he let her go. "Send im away Terra or next time I drop in I'll not be so gentle with ya." he warned before he slipped once more into the shadows. She heard him moving about in the bath and struggled with the urge to be ill.

She'd not give into the terror that tore at her until he was gone.

"Until next time luv," he murmured before he moved to touch her once more. The sound of a gun being cocked cut through the darkness.

"Touch her Kieran and so help me it'll be the last move you ever make," Vince hissed through the shadows.

"Mr. Fenton I was beginning ta wonder if you're skills had dulled with time. I'm glad ta see they haven't."

"Are you okay?" Vince asked.

"Yeah, he was just leavin."

"We've a reckonin ya and I, Mr. Fenton."

"Bring it on."

"Not yet Vince I have business ta finish with Terra Anne first. When our game has played out then and only then will I be comin for ya."

"She told you she was out."

"It doesn't work that way Mr. Fenton and ya know it; I'd imagine."

"It does now."

"Do ya think ya can spare her from mi wrath?"

"I can and I will," Vince said as he flexed his muscles in his finger beginning to pull the trigger.

"Easy there Vince. If ya do that your sweet Lady of the Night's brains will be decoratin the wall before ya do finish mi."

Vince eased his hold on the gun. "I'm not going to shoot now let her go," Vince snapped.

"Good man, a shame ya turned out to be an enemy agent," Kieran said with regret. "I'll be in touch Terra," he breathed before he shoved her in Vince's direction and slipped out of the loft through the skylight.

"Why did you let him in?"

"He'd have broken in and there'd have been consequences for not doing as he said."

"When did he arrange the meet?"

"On the ride home via text."

"Why didn't you say anything?"

"I told ya, I can handle him."

"It looked to me like he was handling you," Vince said with disgust as he moved out of the shadows to her side and noted the bruise that was beginning to form on her cheek. "I can't protect you if you tie my hands."

"I won't risk your life needlessly."

"What did he do to you Terra? I've never known you to fear a threat."

"I learned Kieran doesn't threaten. He does what he says he will."

"What did he come here for?"

"Ta convince mi ta send ya on your way."

"That won't happen."

"Vince..."

"Don't I'm not leaving Terra and if my being close to you will draw him out to face me all the better." Vince stated as he locked the sky light. Terra studied him through the darkness wondering how much he'd heard and seen before he moved in to help her. She figured if he'd caught Kieran kissing her the other man would be dead and she'd be answering about a million questions she wasn't ready to. She watched as he dragged over the chair from her desk and settled into the shadows near her bed.

She'd wanted a moment to herself to recover from what had just happened but Vince wasn't going to give her it. With a resigned sigh she sank down in the bed once more and closed her eyes, she hoped that having him there would keep the nightmares that haunted her at times like this at bay.

Vince watched as Terra settled into her bed once more and kept his gun trained on the sky light from within the shadows where he lay in wait. As he watched her he tried to sort out what he'd walked in on. He'd woken to the smell of blood in the air and crept up the steps in silence when he'd reached the second floor he'd heard her whisper. "All I have to do is scream." her threat was answered by Kieran's of pulling the trigger. A long silence had hung in the air before her mentor spoke again. "Send im away Terra or next time I drop in on ya I won't be so gentle." Vince wondered what that meant but pushed it aside. He'd used the other man's moving off as his chance to move into position. He'd watched as Kieran moved toward Terra again and seeing his intent to touch her had reacted. He'd been ready to fire until Kieran threatened her.

Vince wondered now that the other man was gone just what that strange silence that had occurred was about and why Terra was so afraid of Kieran; she'd actually done as he told her. Both letting the assassin in and then trying to get him to leave her as Kieran demanded. He hoped the answers he needed would be forthcoming soon, be it from her or Jake.

Terra woke as the sunlight poured in the loft under the shades. She blinked as the harsh light hit her eyes. The sound of movement had her rolling out of bed to her feet, gun ready. The shades were drawn to block out the light and when her vision cleared she found herself face to face with Vince. He was studying her with question. She eased her grip on the gun and drew a relieved breath. "Sorry, one too many scares lately," she muttered as she tossed the gun back on her bed.

"What's going on Terra? I've never seen you like this and I don't like it."

"This isn't the first time Kieran has sat outside mi door watchin mi like this," she confessed.

"I thought you said you'd been off the grid," Vince stated annoyed.

"I was. He's located mi a couple times but this last time when he couldn't find mi I guess he decided ta use Kevin ta draw mi out."

"This was never about the DJ; it was about you."

"No, Jessica was in danger there was no deception in that, Kevin crossed him and he'd use her ta hurt him but he had ta know that by targeting her I'd turn up."

"Why?"

"I owe Kevin a great deal."

"What does he want from you?" Vince asked trying to understand why the other man would go to such considerable lengths to draw her back out.

"He wants mi back in his fold," Terra stated.

"What aren't you telling me?"

"Nothing," she lied knowing if Vince knew everything she wouldn't be able to stop him from going to war with her former mentor turned stalker.

"Now that Kevin and Jessica are in the wind why don't you just leave?"

"I'm done waitin for him ta turn up without warnin. I'm finishin this."

"I guess it's true then," Vince said with a sigh.

"What?"

"Assassins only come out of retirement to finish off their trainers."

"I'm not comin out of retirement. I'm done killin people for a livin. I'm just defendin miself. After this I'll disappear for good."

"No, you won't."

"What makes ya think ya know mi mind Mr. Fenton?"

"I don't, but I know mine and I won't let you just vanish without a trace again."

"Vince..."

"You don't have to run."

"Ya said it yourself I'm a watched name."

"You could come in work for us, with the information you know about Kieran..."

"I told ya once before I..."

"That was then, if you came in I could protect you. You could start a new life without fear of discovery."

"I'll think about it."

Vince nodded. "I'll leave you to rest if you like. I'm going to get some breakfast and get some more equipment. You should be safe enough now that it's daylight," he whispered before he drew her to him and kissed her. Terra struggled in his grasp aware Kieran had to be watching. But Vince would not be denied and it wasn't long before her halfhearted efforts to get away changed to a demand of her own.

Her lips came alive under his and vied for control as hands that had been trying to push him away fisted in his hair and clothes drawing him closer. She cursed him and herself for her inability to deny the passion that still existed between them. It had been five years since she last let him touch her. She shouldn't be so eager for him but it seemed that despite logic the fire that burned in her for Vince Fenton had never gone out.

Vince groaned as the heat of her kiss hit him like a gut shot and left him weak with need for her. His hands pawed at her body through her clothes and she purred with delight as she tore at his clothes seeking skin. He followed her lead hands fisting around her night shirt to pull it off and she brushed his hands away stopping him denying him the right to do so. When he reached for her again she broke their kiss and eased back.

"Terra?" he questioned confused and more than just a little frustrated.

"I'm sorry Vince but I'm not ready for this," she muttered as she smoothed out his mussed hair.

"You could have fooled me," he said with irritation.

"Bein ready physically isn't the same as bein ready," she reminded.

Vince nodded. He knew it was true and if she hadn't come to terms with what had happened before then he didn't want to push her hand. They needed to get past the hurt and mistrust or anything they started would be short lived and that wasn't what he wanted. "Fair enough, I'll go see about breakfast and then we'll sort out the rest of the day before you go to the station."

"Sounds good," she said gratitude shown in her eyes for his giving her the space she was requesting.

"I won't be long. When I get back I want to talk about before."

"Okay," she relented. He was right they needed to talk through everything between them before anything else happened. She watched as he left before sinking back down into her bed aware that she didn't have a whole lot longer she could hold off on revealing all to him. She could never keep anything hidden from him for long.

She'd not been alone for long before she heard the front door open. She smiled amused. "What's the matter Mr. Fenton did that last kiss make ya forget your wallet or somethin?" She teased. She waited for his reply but none came. Sitting up she opened her eyes. "Vince?" She questioned as she reached for her gun.

It was a moment later she heard the sickening pop of electrical fuses being triggered as the trap Vince had set was activated. She cursed aware that it was Kieran and not Vince in the house. Getting to her feet she watched with a sick horror and fascination as flames bloomed on the walls below and began to rapidly spread toward the second floor. She spotted Kieran in the center of the room his gray eyes glowed with rage as he watched the loft around him go up in flame.

She smiled it seemed Vince's trap had worked perfectly Kieran was a rat in a trap, too bad she was there as well. Rising from the bed she began the task of finding a way out.

Vince turned the corner from the light to Terra's street; his gear in tow along with breakfast. He was picturing her reaction to this morning's pastry of choice when he first heard the sirens. As he rounded the corner to the street that her loft was on, his heart skipped a beat; the emergency vehicles were gathered on her lawn. Her loft burning out of control. It looked like Kieran had tried to make his move and wound up springing his trap, with Terra still in the loft.

Vince got out of his x-runner and moved towards the house.

"Sir you have to stay back; it's not safe."

"Was there anyone in there?"

"I don't know. Neighbors claim the woman who lives there was inside but we haven't found anyone yet. It's too hot to go inside."

"Did anyone see her come out?"

"No sir, no one saw anything?'

Vince pulled out his phone to punch in her number and cursed realizing he didn't have it. He dialed the number he'd been given for Kevin and waited for the cop to answer but got a voice mail and cursed. He punched in the man's number a second time and pounced the moment the other man picked up.

"Kevin, its Vince, I need Terra's number, now."

"Are those sirens I hear?"

"I haven't got time for questions Kevin I need that number."

"Why, what's happened?"

"Kieran tried to break in the loft he set off my trap with Terra inside; I need to know if she got clear."

"Shit."

Vince listened as the other man rattled off the number before he hung up and punched it in.

The phone went to voice mail and he growled with frustration. "Terra Anne, it' Vince, if you get this call me, immediately, I need to know you're alright."

Vince got back in his truck and drove back out of the

neighborhood aware that if he was still there when the cops turned up he'd be detained for questioning and right now he couldn't risk being detained. Part of him wanted to stay and confirm if Terra was in the loft or not but if she'd gotten out then she would need him to either pick her up or take care of any injury she may have sustained due to the blaze. As he punched in her number again he cursed himself for a fool; aware that his trap may have cost him the one person in the world he didn't want to lose.

It was a little after sunset when Vince gave up looking for her and headed back to his hotel. His check on the status of the blaze listed it as contained but no word was forth coming as to if any survivors had been identified or any bodies. Vince dialed Terra's number again and his heart sank as the familiar recording played yet again. As he mounted the steps he wished for the sensation of being watched. Longed for Kieran to take the shot he'd been threatening him with for two days and end him. He deserved no less, after all, he'd contributed to her death.

Vince swallowed back guilt and grief as he stepped into his room. He crossed to the fridge, his mind set on a drink. He didn't bother with the lights, the dark matched his mood.

"We really need ta exchange numbers Vince," a familiar voice said through the darkness.

Vince turned to the bed his eyes searching for the source of the voice wondering if he'd finally gone mad. "Terra Anne."

"Yeah. I heard the door open thought it was ya. Realized it was im when I heard the fuses go on your trap. Took some effort but I managed ta get out the skylight. My phone is toast though. I picked up the phone here once I got in ta call ya and realized I didn't know your number. I've been waiting for ya ta get back ever since," she said amused.

Vince was at her side, instantly, his hands cupping her face studying her as if he didn't believe his eyes. "Are you okay?" he asked.

She nodded as she became aware he wasn't. "Ya didn't think I was..."

His mouth covered hers cutting off the question unable to even hear the word as it was exactly what he'd thought. He took now without mercy unable to hold back the hunger that tore through him.

He was desperate to touch her if only to assure himself she was real. His hands tore open her jeans and were pulling them off as he joined her in the bed. His fingers had her lower half bare within moments. Terra watched dazed and defenseless as he unfastened his belt and shed his own slacks. His hands pawed over her thighs setting off a spark of need inside of her that left her breathless before he pressed inside her filling her depths.

Terra gasped at the feeling of him inside of her but she didn't draw away, only held him to her; aware that reason had left him. He'd thought her gone and he needed her this way to quiet his troubled mind. She drew him deeper and whispered his name assuring him that she was real and he was wanted. He linked their hands and kissed her once more as he began to move inside her. With each advance he drove the image of the loft burning out of control from his mind and with every caress of her body his fear subsided.

Vince opened his eyes to take in the sight of her beneath him and he trembled. Those haunting green eyes stared back at him full of compassion and desire; it humbled him as sanity returned. He recalled that they'd agreed to talk about everything between them before they took this step. He wanted that, a clean slate between them and he knew she'd been looking for the same. She'd needed time to work through it all. They would have that talk but it would wait. His eyes conveyed his apology for the change in plans and she kissed him to assure him that it was okay, she understood. His eyes fell shut and he lost himself in the feel of her.

Terra kissed tears from his eyes, she figured he was unaware of, and trembled beneath him; stunned by the intensity of the emotion riding him. She'd seen in his eyes that clarity had returned and she could tell from his pace that he was trying to regain his control and she was relieved. Vince was not one prone to letting his emotions get the better of him.

When they'd been together in Belfast he'd always talked to her about not getting emotionally invested in a job. Compartmentalizing her feelings so that she didn't lose control of a situation. The man who'd walked in the door had been anything but that cool and collected agent. He was still shaken but recovering quickly.

As she fell over the edge into bliss she felt him follow and was stunned by it; Vince had never, not been able to wait her out and go again. That he'd gone over with her said much for his mental state. She ran her hands over his skin and held him close as his body grew weak from release. "Shh, I've got ya," she murmured as she kissed his head where it lay on her still covered breast.

"I thought I'd killed you," he said weakly giving voice to the fear that had ripped him apart for the last several hours.

"I'm fine Vince," she assured him.

"I got there; the flat was an inferno..."

"It went up like a roman candle the trap worked perfectly," she assured him.

"Nobody saw anyone get out. The fire department wouldn't let me get close enough to see anything, it was too hot they couldn't get in to verify if anyone was..."

"I made it out."

"I called Kevin for your number then tried it and all I kept getting was your voice mail. I looked for you..."

"My phone was still in the loft. I came straight here figured it was safe. If Kieran managed to slip out as well I didn't want ta be on the street. I was goin ta call ya but..."

"You didn't have my number. I'll make sure you do from now on," he whispered before he kissed her face.

"I figured when ya didn't find mi you'd come here. I never thought you'd think that. I'm sorry."

"Not your fault," he murmured as he kissed her hair followed by her eyebrows and lids. "I never should have left you alone."

"It's not yours either. Kieran did this not ya. If that trap hadn't been there..."

"I'm glad you're okay," he breathed before he kissed her again. She kissed him back gently and then drew away.

"I hate ta cut this short Mr. Fenton but I've got ta get ta the station."

Vince nodded noting the time. "Five minutes," he requested.

She smiled and nodded before brushing his cheek with a kiss and sliding out of the bed. She picked up her jeans and moved into the bathroom to get ready to go. Vince lay in his bed and tried to find his balance. He'd lost control. It was unsettling but the fear that had held him, until he saw her, had him in a strangle hold. He'd not believed her real until their eyes met.

The fevered need that had burned in him had raged as out of control, as the loft he'd thought she died in. He'd wanted her; he still wanted her. It took every ounce of his strength to not slip out of the bed and go after her. He sat up in the bed; disgusted to find he'd not even finished shedding his own clothes. His slacks were still bunched around his hips and his shirt like hers still on. He'd not been so impatient to have a woman since he was a reckless teenager. He'd behaved like a stag in rut. It was a wonder she hadn't smacked him

Vince grumbled as he fixed his pants.

When Terra reemerged from the bathroom he was dressed and ready to go. She moved past him without a word and headed to the door. He moved past her and opened the door looking down the hall for any signs of movement before giving her the nod to come ahead. He led her to his truck and issued her inside, once she was secure he slid in behind the steering wheel and pulled into traffic headed for the station.

5 FRIDAY

Thursday passed by in a blur. The evening at the station uneventful. When they made it back to the hotel they'd both been too tired to do little more than crawl into bed. It was a little after four am when Vince woke to the sensation of being watched. He eased his hold on Terra and lifted his head careful not to wake her. As he slipped out of the bed he grabbed his phone and made his way outside.

The moment he set foot on the balcony his phone rang. He pressed the button to connect the line and was keenly aware once more of being caught in the cross hairs of Kieran's rifle.

"That was a mighty fine trap ya left for mi, Mr. Fenton. I was glad ta hear Terra Anne made it out of there as well. Not so happy ta find the two of ya wrapped around each other again I warned her ta stay away from ya."

"She's done playing your games Kieran."

"Is that so?"

"She's not interested in your job. Terra Anne is retired leave her be."

"Is that what ya think this about Mr. Fenton a job? I see mi lady has learned ta keep secrets at last. Good for her."

"She said you came to hire her back. What else would there be?" Vince asked his voice impatient.

"Ya might better ask Terra that first."

"I won't leave her again Kieran so I suggest you leave. This is the only chance you'll get."

"That's right kind of ya Mr. Fenton but I've no intention of leavin without Terra Anne so I suggest ya rethink your offer."

"When I find you..."

"Temper Vince? I've never known ya ta be emotional. Perhaps ya've spent too much time with Terra. I wonder what your superiors would think of your bunkin up with a former killer and your old lover."

"I'm on vacation they wouldn't much care," Vince bluffed he hated to even think how they might react if it became public knowledge he was with Terra again.

"I doubt that. Watch your step Mr. Fenton or you'll lose a lot more than just your control," Kieran warned before he hung up the phone.

Vince studied his cell phone with puzzlement as he wondered how the other man had gotten his number. He shook his head it didn't matter. With deliberate strides he returned to the bed and lay back down with Terra. Making it clear he was going nowhere.

They slept the day away exhausted by the previous day's events. When they woke it was a little before seven. Vince had no time to ask her about his conversation with Kieran that morning as after changing they'd departed for the station.

Once more Vince took post outside the booth and listened as Terra hosted the request show. It had been on but a few minutes when Kieran's voice cut over the airwaves.

"Does he know about us yet, mi darling, Terra Anne your Mr. Fenton?"

"There's nothing to tell." she said with disinterest.

"Mr. Fenton might not see it that way lass. Men are a funny lot. We tend ta take this sort of thing very serious."

"It's enough Kieran," Terra snapped in warning forgetting about using the stage name. He was saying too much.

"Na, not yet. I went ta pay your cop friend a visit this morning but ta mi disappointment he was gone. Do ya think ya can hide im and his pretty lady friend from mi luv."

"Ya needn't concern yourself with im. He's no one. I'm the one who put ya in jail." She reminded.

"Yeah, that ya are. Fine, I'll let them go but it'll cost ya Terra Anne and for tryin to hide im there will be a reprisal."

"I figured as much."

"We'll discuss this further luv when your Mr. Fenton isn't listenin in. Till then remember *I won't let ya go, my baby*," he murmured before the line broke signaling he'd hung up. Terra cued up the George Michael song and tried not to tremble. "I never should have come out of hidin," she whispered with dismay.

As soon as the song was rolling she heard the door to the booth thrown open. Looking up she saw Vince. He stared back at her with barely contained fury and she fought for calm.

"What the hell was he talking about?"

"Nothin, like I said."

"It didn't sound like nothing. It sounded like he was suggesting that you and he were..." Vince began but she cut him off.

"I don't care what it sounded like. I'm tellin ya it's nothin."

"Were you involved with him after I left?" Vince asked with disgust.

"No," her answer came instantly the word harsh and vehement.

"Then why is he sayin he owns ya? Men don't say things like that unless..."

"He made mi Vince, it's his right to end mi as well," Terra said her voice shaking with fear. She cursed mentally aware that Kieran was getting to her.

"The hell it is! I don't ever want to hear you say that again Terra Anne. Do you hear me?" Vince snarled as he grabbed her by the arm and shook her.

Terra flinched in reflex and regretted it instantly as he saw it and in seeing it began to put the pieces together. "Did he..." Vince swallowed unable to get the last words past his lips. The thought of it to terrible to utter.

He didn't have to. He saw it in her eyes as he struggled to say it and his stomach churned with disgust. Rage boiled in him with no place to go. Terra was his, if he got his hands on Kieran...

Vince's hands coiled tight and he heard Terra gasp. He blinked realizing he was still holding her arm. He let her go seeing the bite marks on her ivory skin where his nails had dug in. "I'm sorry," he whispered with regret not just for scaring her but for not being there to protect her.

"Don't... it wasn't your fault."

"I shouldn't have left you."

"If you'd stayed he'd have killed ya and I'd have still been punished. What good would that have done? At least this way you're here now."

"I could have taken you with me," Vince argued giving voice to a thought that had dogged him for five years.

"Na, ya couldn't. Your people wouldn't have taken ta kindly ta your protection of a known killer I'd wager."

"Where does Kevin fit in to this?" Vince asked unable to hold the question at bay. Unable to forget the exchange between them.

"He was the officer that found mi after Kieran was done with mi.

He handled me case."

"Nothing else?"

"Nothing."

"But he hugged you. I saw closeness..."

"Na, I hugged him. Nobody gets close ta mi unless I let um."

Vince replayed the meet in his mind and cursed. She had initiated contact even with the kiss he'd bestowed on her brow she'd tilted her head to him to receive it.

"You were more than an asset to me Terra Anne."

"Aye and ya were more than mi friend."

"I'm glad we got that straight," he muttered with a half grin.

"I think it's about time we sorted out the rest as well Mr. Fenton." She whispered.

"When you're ready, Terra Anne."

She nodded before she leaned into him and brushed his lips with her own. Vince's response was pure instinct born from years of wanting. His hands sank into her hair fisting in the dark locks, breaking up curls as his mouth came alive under hers taking greedily.

Terra gasped shocked by the jolt of hunger he awoke in her and he groaned with need as he fought for control knowing if he moved too soon she'd spook.

"Vince," she breathed his name with that seductive voice that went out over the airwaves and it was nearly his undoing.

"Ah, hell Terra you've got to stop love; I want to touch you too much," Vince muttered as he ended their kiss.

"Put your hands on me Vince," she demanded more than ready for him.

Vince's hands slid free of her hair to take hold of her hips. He dragged her body against his so that there was no space between them but it wasn't enough. He needed more of her. He longed to have her naked and trembling with desire for him. He wanted to be inside her again, to feel her wet heat mold around him as he filled her and drove her wild with the pleasure of it.

As he gave her what she'd asked Vince opened his eyes wanting to see her response to him as he built her arousal. He'd dreamed of this more nights than he cared to admit over the last five years and couldn't resist the urge. When his eyes opened he realized that they weren't in the privacy of his hotel but in the booth at the station. Glancing at the clock he noted the time and groaned she wasn't done with the broadcast and after the last call if she wasn't at the mike on cue, security would be in instantly.

With disappointment he eased back. He watched as green eyes

opened, in their depths were hurt and confusion.

"Not now Terra Anne you're still on the air," he stated.

She blinked dumbfounded as his words sank in and then laughed. "I'd forgotten where we were," she admitted with a blush. "For a moment I was back in our little flat in Belfast."

"So, had I; as much as I want to get you out of those clothes right now I know if you don't come back on air on cue we'll be interrupted."

Terra nodded. Vince brushed a kiss on her forehead before he turned and moved back to his post outside the door.

"Aloha Kauai we're closing in on the witching hour and my time at the ball is almost up but I've got time for just a few more calls. If there's a special someone out there you want to send out a song to give me a call. For now here's my nightly dedication. This one is from your Lady of the Night to that special someone out there," She purred before cueing up the song *(Meredith Brooks What would happen if we kiss).*

Vince groaned the woman was going to kill him after all. It would be a new one on the record books; elite spy assassinated, cause of death, sexual frustration.

When the show ended Vince lead his charge from the building to his truck. She slid into the passenger seat without a word and waited for him to make his move. To her disbelief he didn't touch her. He started the engine and sped for his hotel. She shifted in her seat uncomfortable, her body still dangerously aroused from their encounter in the booth. Temper flared inside her; how could he ignore her like this. She wanted him to distraction and he seemed unaware of it.

It was maddening. He wasn't going to act like nothing had happened earlier; she wouldn't let him. She'd meant what she said it was time to sort things out between them. Once they got inside she was going to remind him.

Vince followed Terra up the steps and in the door of his hotel room careful to keep his distance, he wasn't going to initiate contact as it seemed to frighten her. He didn't want her scared, he wanted her uninhibited. When she was ready he'd follow her lead.

He didn't wait long the second the door was shut Terra drew him against her. Her mouth crashed into his wild and demanding. He answered her with the same heat drawing her against him. He lost himself in her kiss until he noted the open blinds. He drew back a second time and she growled with displeasure.

"Not here Terra. I won't share you with him; not even a glimpse."

Terra nodded but in a show of refusal to let go she wrapped her legs around his waist. Vince carried her to the bed behind the door. She slid down his body putting her feet on the floor before she tore open his shirt wanting to feel his skin under her fingers.

Vince reached to pull off hers and she stopped him.

"Not that, not yet," she breathed desperate for him, but she wasn't ready for him to see the extent of her punishment at Kieran's hand. It would only bring questions interrupting them again.

Vince nodded turning his focus to her skirt. It slid to the floor and she stepped out of it without hesitation taking a step toward him and the bed as her own hands worked to pull his belt free of his jeans.

Vince's hands slid down shapely hips his fingers traced along the elastic bands of her panties raising goose flesh in their wake. Her hips arched toward his touch and his hand dipped beneath the thin layer to touch her silky thighs. When his hand brushed over her feminine mound she moaned with need. He answered her cry by driving a skilled finger into her heated depths. He smirked to find her wet and ready for him. Oh yeah, this was His Terra, Vince thought with satisfaction. He watched as her eyes flew open startled by his intrusion so soon and he cursed realizing he'd moved too fast. He drew the invading digit out of her slowly.

"Stay with me Terra Anne, we're just getting started," he murmured needing her to relax. Knowing if he didn't have her now after earlier he'd go mad.

Terra unfastened his jeans and pushed them off his hips. Her nails scraped over his skin lightly as she exposed his thighs and calves. She bit her lip at the sight of him before her. If it were possible he looked to be in better shape now than before.

The wicked hand he'd slipped in her underwear was wreaking havoc on her system. Pressing against sensitive flesh that was now screaming for his full attention. His nails raking over and through spiky feminine curls; fingers teasing her depths where he'd drove into too soon making them ache for his return but not pressing in since the first shocking jolt.

Terra shifted under his touch restless and impatient ready for more.

"I'm with ya," she assured him.

Vince taking her hint gave her what she craved plunging his

finger in her once more but slower and deeper this time. He watched with approval as her eyes fell shut once more and she lost herself in the pleasure his touch gave her.

All too quickly though he found that touching her wasn't enough. It never was with Terra. His aroused flesh strained within its confines for its turn to fill her. Slowly he peeled away the thin layer of silk that kept her from him. The hand that teased her with slow lazy caresses became more insistent with its efforts taking the slow burn he'd begun to build inside her to a raging fire letting her know his intent.

Terra gasped and her eyes opened to meet with his once more. A wicked smile curved her succulent lips.

"Why are ya so impatient Mr. Fenton?" She purred as her soft, slender feminine hand reached into his boxers and gave his balls a light squeeze.

Vince groaned as his head fell back and his eyes closed involuntarily in response to her touch.

"It's been too long Mrs. Fenton," he murmured before his mouth covered hers once more, claiming it with a kiss that stole her breath away and consumed her marking her as his. She answered him in kind as her slow walk had his knees bumping the end of the bed. She gave him another good squeeze that had him falling back on the mattress. She laughed at the sight of him there. "No one's called mi that in five years," she said amused. "If you'd waited another two they'd have declared ya legally dead," she muttered with annoyance. "Why didn't ya come back?"

"I did. But you'd already left," he admitted.

"Ya could have come after mi," she muttered.

"I didn't think I'd be welcome."

"Ya were."

"I'm here now," he reminded.

"That ya are."

"Terra please if you mean to have me then get over here otherwise shoot me and get it over with it'll be less painful," he groused.

Terra laughed again. She'd known when she saw him in the hotel room that first night it would come to this. She'd not craved another since he left. She was his. In a way their time together had branded her so. Even if he'd never come back she knew she'd have never touched another. "I've no use for ya dead Vince. There are things I want from ya that require ya ta be breathin," she teased as she moved toward him.

"But aye, you're right it's been too long." she whispered as she pulled his boxers off leaving him naked before her. Terra bit her lip in hunger at the site of him and then joined him on the bed. Her hips straddled his thighs pressing the part of her that made them one against the source of his need. Vince groaned fingers clenching around the sheets as she shifted above him taking him in.

As she lowered herself on him she saw him strain with the need to take control of the moment. She smiled before she pulled off her shirt revealing the last of her body to him. Before she lowered herself to rest her head against his chest. Vince kissed her before he took the control she offered. Turning them so she lay beneath him. He held her close for a moment before he began to move. Driving them both towards release.

6 SATURDAY

Vince woke a little before sunrise with a jolt. An unpleasant dream faded from his mind forgotten as he felt the warm body wrapped about him. Terra. She was safe. He wasn't sure exactly how they'd ended up together in his hotel as the past few days felt like a blur after five years apart. She'd been slow to let him back in but once she had let him touch her something had shifted between them. She'd not let him go since. Each time she felt him withdrawing from her she'd drawn him back to her again and he'd been unable to leave her.

There were things he needed to be doing to prepare for the fall out of last night's turn of events he'd wanted to get an early start but she'd kept him from it. Now as he looked upon her he wondered how he'd managed to be apart from her as long as he had. Hungry eyes roamed over her face, studying every line and curve as they moved down her neck the morning light began to peak through the blinds. Dark lashes fluttered before green eyes shot open. She wrapped the sheet about her tight hiding herself from him.

Vince watched her with concern and noted the moment panic left her and she relaxed. "Morning," he whispered.

She breathed his name with relief before she kissed him.

"How are you feeling?" he asked as he broke their kiss.

"Famished," she admitted.

"I'll see about breakfast, get dressed after we eat we'll need to talk about how to handle Kieran."

Terra nodded and watched as Vince slipped out of the bed. Pulling on his slacks he moved into the kitchen area to fix coffee. She picked up her clothes and moved into the bathroom to freshen up.

Vince was in the process of heating water when his phone rang. Drawing the cell from his pocket he noted the number and smiled it seemed Jake had finally come through with the Intel he'd requested.

"Hello."

"Vince, I got that info you wanted but it wasn't easy. Are you sure you want to hear this, it's grim."

"Yeah, I'm sure."

"Okay, but don't say I didn't warn you. I've got a police report and a medical file; which do you want first?"

"Give me the medical."

"When emergency arrived on scene she was dead they revived her and she died again in transit to the hospital. Upon arrival she was treated for multiple stab wounds to the chest. Head injury, broken bones and internal bleeding; just to list a few of her more pronounced injuries."

"Don't sugar coat it Jake I want details."

"Why?"

"The bastard is going to pay for every bruise, cut, broken bone and harm he dealt her. When I get my hands on him he's going to wish she'd just shot him."

"Vince…"

"If you haven't got the stomach to read it then send it to me I'll read it myself," Vince snapped with irritation.

"Fine you want it you got it I had nightmares after reading that thing."

"Thank you Jake."

"You may not be so eager to thank me once you get it Vince. You're lady friend got worked over but good by this Kieran jerk."

"Yeah, I got some of it from her last night but I appreciate the warning."

"Watch your back Vince this guy is a real piece of work."

"Will do."

"If you want back up let me know."

"I appreciate the offer but this one is unsanctioned I don't want to land you in trouble."

"Right, well, uh, happy hunting then," Jake muttered before he hung up.

Vince turned his focus to the message center on his blackberry and opened the file Jake had sent. As he began to read his gaze moved to the bathroom checking that Terra was not yet out. He read the report to himself and understood why Jake had been reluctant to read it aloud. The news was grim, worse than Vince had even been picturing. He could understand why Terra was so guarded. Kieran, the man who had trained her as an assassin and she'd looked at as a father, had beaten, raped and tortured her before leaving her for dead. Vince cursed understanding why Terra referred to the man as an oath -breaker.

Vince closed the file as Terra emerged from the bathroom dressed in one of the hotel robes. He noticed the fear from the past few days beginning to settle in again and felt his temper flare. The Terra he'd known had been fearless and wild; the woman before him now was guarded and hesitant. Timid even and he hated it. Aware that his anger would only serve to upset her further Vince decided he needed to get out of there. As he grabbed his keys he watched Terra's eyes fill with questions.

"I'm going to get some cream for your coffee and something from the bakery I'll be back soon," he assured her before brushing a kiss on her forehead and walking out.

Terra watched as Vince walked out of the hotel room with a growing sense of unease. The last time he'd left under a pretense had been five years ago and he'd not come back. He'd received word from the agency he worked for his cover was compromised and left her to swing in the wind. He'd left her to face Kieran's wrath.

"That isn't what's happening now," she muttered to herself as her cell phone rang. Terra lifted it to her ear and pressed the button to connect the call. "Hello," she said in a distracted greeting.

"Top of the Mornin' to ya Terra-Ann mi darlin' and how are ya feelin this fine morn?" Kieran asked his voice calm and polite.

"I'm doin just fine Kieran despite the fire ball ya almost killed us with."

"That was not meant to happen mi luv. I figure I have your dear Mr. Fenton ta thank for that. "

"Aye it was his trap," she confirmed.

"A right good one it was too. He always was good with explosives your man."

"That he is."

"Did ya get a good night's sleep there Terra-Ann I'd hate for ya ta sound worn over the radio tonight."

"I slept just fine."

"That's good. I see your Mr. Fenton is out and about early this morin. What is it he's up ta today I wonder?"

"Getting breakfast," Terra stated.

"He seems in a mighty big hurry, perhaps he's tryin' ta skip town on ya again."

"He wouldn't do that," Terra snapped with more certainty than she felt.

"Ya don't sound so sure of that Terra mi darlin' and of course how can I blame ya I mean he left ya before and look what happened," Kieran mocked.

"He's coming back," Terra stated.

"We'll see luv," Kieran answered before he hung up on her.

Terra put down her phone and settled down onto the couch. She flipped on the TV to pass the time while she awaited Vince's return. \

Vince stepped out of the bakery with breakfast in tow. His neck itched with the unsettling feel of Kieran's cross hairs on his back. He'd been aware of the assassin watching him since he stepped out of the hotel and he seethed inside with the need to strike down the man who'd dare harm his wife.

"Come down from your perch you bastard and let's end this," Vince muttered under his breath as he made his way toward his truck. As soon as he got behind the wheel he took off hoping to spot Kieran tailing him but the guy was good. Not following too long or passing to often if he was behind him Vince didn't see him.

Noting the time and figuring Terra would begin to worry Vince gave up the hunt turning the truck in the direction of the hotel.

When he stepped out into the lot the cross hairs were back and he cursed. It seemed Kieran had opted to just head back to the hotel. As he made his way toward the lobby entrance his phone rang. Vince pressed the button for speaker phone and then connected the line.

"Kieran."

"Mr. Fenton did ya enjoy all your windin about?"

"Yeah gave me a chance to clear my head," Vince replied.

"That's good but I don't imagine it relaxed sweet Terra any. I think she's worried ya ran off again."

"I won't be leaving her again Kieran."

"That's good ta hear Mr. Fenton I'm sure it will give Terra-Ann a good deal of relief ta hear it."

"What do you want Kieran we both know you didn't call to make small talk?"

"Quite right. I thought it was sweet really seeing ya fall apart like ya did thinkin' ya'd killed her. I was less than amused though when ya blinded me ta her movements. I like ta keep a close eye on mi girl."

"Well you best get used to it Kieran because you're never going to get another glimpse at my wife again." Vince snapped in defiance.

Kieran laughed at the display. A sickening soulless sound that chilled Vince to the bone. "Ya can't keep her from mi Vince."

"Watch me."

"You're a fool ta try. She's mine."

"The hell she is. I know what you did to her Kieran and when I get my hands on you; you'll pay," Vince hissed before he broke the call. As he reached for the front door his phone rang a second time. He mashed the button. "What?" He demanded of the other man.

He heard the familiar and sickening pop of a suppressed gun a moment before he felt the sharp pain of the snipers fire tear through his flesh. ". We're not finished yet."

"Yes, we are."

"If ya hang up on mi again Terra will suffer for it."

"I'm listening."

"Don't ever presume ta cut me off again Mr. Fenton."

"I won't," Vince assured him aware that Kieran was holding his control by a thread.

"That's better, now I suggest ya listen and listen well. Terra-Ann is mine yank and if ya don't back off it will cost ya dearly."

Vince held his bloody arm applying pressure to slow the loss of blood as he looked for where the assassin had fired from. "Is that really how you want to end this Kieran a quick pop and the smell of gun powder; no risk involved at all? Are you a coward then after all? Afraid to face me man to man."

"The shot was a warnin Vince next time we speak it'll be face ta face when I take Terra-Ann from ya for good." Kieran hissed before he disconnected the call.

Vince put away his phone before entering the hotel. He let out the breath he'd been unaware of holding before moving through the lobby for the elevator careful to avoid drawing attention to himself.

Terra switched off the TV as Vince stepped into the room. As she moved to greet him she noted the blood staining his sleeve and winced. "What happened?"

"I made Kieran mad," Vince muttered.

"That was a dumb thing ta do Mr. Fenton. You're lucky he didn't just kill ya."

"I talked him out of it," Vince said with a cocky smirk that both infuriated her and excited her.

"Ya always were a manipulative son of a bitch when it suited ya," Terra teased as she led him over to the couch.

"I prefer persuasive."

Terra unbuttoned the cuff of his shirt and rolled it up to inspect the wound. "It's a clean shot went through. I don' know about ya Mr. Fenton but I'm right tired of this prick. I think it's time I drew him out."

"Terra I don't think that's a good idea. The last time you faced him he nearly killed you," Vince breathed as he drew open the collar of her bathrobe to reveal the scars Kieran had left on her. "Did you think you had to hide them from me? That I'd find you any less desirable if I saw them."

"Yes... no, maybe... I don't know." She muttered as she tried to cover them once more.

"There's no shame in these Terra-Ann. They're proof he didn't break you."

"He came close." Terra whispered.

"I know. You died twice in transit to the hospital and thrice more once you got there. I don't want to give him the chance to finish what he started."

"I understand, but ya need ta see that if I don't face him now I'll be runnin from the bastard forever." Terra related.

Vince cursed with displeasure knowing she was right. "What did you have in mind?"

Terra smiled pleased to have won the argument. She fixed her robe before turning her undivided attention to his injured arm. As she tended to the wound she laid out her plan for him.

Vince struggled to hold back his objections and just listen. The plan as she laid it out was solid and well thought out; it would work. Under normal circumstances it was exactly how he'd have run the op but this was his wife he was risking and he was hesitant to put her in harm's way.

"It's a good plan, I don't like it, but I'll get over it. For it to work he's going to have to believe every part of the set up and it won't be easy. He's aware of my agency affiliations which means he may look for the trap." Vince warned.

"As long as we play it true ta the past he'll buy it hook line and sinker. When he called earlier he eluded ta your leaving as if he's waiting for it ta happen."

"Then let's give him what he wants and make him regret it," Vince said. He may not like the idea of using her as bait but he wanted to end this thing and soon.

Terra nodded and gave him a quick kiss. "Thank you."

"Don't thank me yet Terra you may wish we hadn't done this by the time it's over," he warned knowing that the game they were about to play might end up reopening old wounds.

"I won't let it get ta mi," she assured him

"I need a couple hours to set things up on my end. I just hope I can get the support I need," Vince muttered before he moved into the guest room to get to work.

He picked up his phone and sliding the key pad out typed a brief text to his second. He hoped that she was still willing to accommodate him in his efforts to rescue Terra Anne, otherwise his part in the next phase of the hunt may prove impossible to pull off.

Vince paced the floor of his room in a display of nerves as he waited for the goddess's response. When his phone chimed, he swallowed back his fear that it would be a refusal and picking up the cell he pressed the key to retrieve the message. Seeing the reply he smiled. Then he sent a brief explanation of what he needed. With the pieces in place he moved back into the main room of the suite. Terra looked up from the TV she'd been watching, her green eyes full of questions.

Vince crossed the room to her side. He drew her close to him and whispered in her ear. "We're all set; everything is in place on my end."

She nodded her understanding and whispered a thank you, which he cut off as his lips met with hers. He had no desire for her thanks and no interest in the reminder of the plan that they were setting into motion. A war raged inside his mind as he fought against his every instinct that told him not to leave her.

The kiss turned rough as he drew her against him demanding her surrender. She melted in his embrace and he felt his stomach churn with disgust at the thought of what would come next. His hands played over her body taking mild arousal to painful need as he tore through her every defense against him like a hurricane. He felt her hands grab his head nails bighting his scalp as she fought for more.

His own body strained with desire demanding he stop teasing

them both and he groaned with hunger as his mouth parted hers to taste whatever skin he could reach. His hands fisted in her shirt and tore it open. Blue eyes lit with excitement as he encountered bare skin rather than a lacy barrier. Damn her she was wearing no bra. Was she trying to kill him, Vince wondered as he stared at her luscious breasts with awe and a burning hunger?

"You're going to pay for that one Terra Anne," he breathed before he lowered his head to her neck and marked the delicate skin. She moaned with pleasure beneath him her hands fisting in his hair.

"Do your worst Mr. Fenton," she demanded as her hands slid free of his hair and down his back to grab his ass and drag him down against her hips. Pressing his aroused flesh against her pelvis eliciting a hiss from him.

Vince grabbed her hands and pinned them to the sofa putting an end to her mischief before he lowered his head to taste the tempting flesh before him. She squirmed beneath him as he teased her with barely there kisses. "Be patient," he whispered with a chuckle before he lowered his head once again as his mouth wrapped around a tight peak to taste it his phone began to ring.

Terra growled in protest as Vince turned away from her to answer the offending object.

"Don't ya dare," she snapped with annoyance.

"Hush lady, I have to take this and you know it," He muttered as he released his hold on her wrists. As he picked up the phone with one hand his other rubbed her thighs distractedly to pacify her and yet keep her ready for him.

"Fenton," he muttered with a small hint of irritation. He half listened to what his second was saying to him as he trapped the phone between his chin and shoulder. Both hands free he unbuttoned Terra's slacks and lowered the zipper. Pulling the offending garment off her hips to bunch around her ankles. He tore the thin wisp of silk exposing her to him and he sucked in a breath at the sight of her naked before him.

"Vince did you hear me? Command is demanding you get your ass back here ASAP. Whatever your DJ is into is not our affair. You've been ordered to leave now or else we'll have no choice but to extract you and deal with your asset for you."

"That won't be necessary; I'm on my way in ten."

"There isn't ten to spare Mr. Fenton chopper leaves in five."

"Damn it, I'm sort of in the middle of something," he muttered with irritation as he turned his focus from his trembling wife to the phone.

"I don't care Mr. Fenton; Get your ass out here now. If your little IRA whore is in the middle of sucking you off, you better push her away, zip up and deal with the blue balls, because if I have to come in there I have authorization to eliminate her."

"You wouldn't dare," Vince hissed with outrage.

"Try me."

"Damn you." Vince cursed before looking over at Terra. "I'm on my way."

"You're leavin?" Terra asked with disbelief and outrage.

"I've got to."

"Ya can't..."

"If I don't your dead."

"Ya do and I am for sure."

"I'm sorry."

Terra flinched. He watched as she crossed her arms over her chest in a bid to reestablish her defenses against him. "You're sorry. I don't believe ya Mr. Fenton. Ya promise mi Kieran won't hurt mi again vow ta protect mi and the moment your damn employer calls ya drop everything and run like a damn dog."

"Terra...." Vince whispered as he reached to comfort her.

"Don't touch mi. Ya make mi sick."

"Terra please let me..."

"Explain, no need I get it. Are ya even coming back?"

"I don't know," he admitted.

"Get out, and don't bother. I'll be fine on mi own. I was happier that way."

"You don't mean that."

"I do. Take this with ya, I don't want it anymore we're done Mr. Fenton," she hissed as she threw her ring at him.

"Terra..."

"I said get out." she roared before she rose from the couch and walked out of the room. Vince moved to follow her but she slammed the door in his face.

"Damn it Terra I don't have time for this, open the door right now or I'll break it down."

"Ya try it and I'll shoot."

"Terra..."

"Go Mr. Fenton I'd hate for ya ta miss your flight."

"I'm coming back," he assured her.

"I won't be here when ya get back," she countered.

"I'll find you again."

"Ya come near me and I'll kill ya."

"You're bluffing."

"Try mi and see."

"I love you."

"Then don't go."

"You know I can't."

"No Mr. Fenton not can't, won't and that's why were done. Your job will always come first."

Vince turned and walked away from the door knowing there was no reasoning with her when she got like this. He'd have to wait her out. With regret he grabbed his bag got in the Toyota x-runner and drove off to meet his contact and catch his flight out of Hawaii.

As he drove he was aware of a tail but made no real effort to shake it. In this case he wanted Kieran to follow him. Needed the other man to believe that he was leaving Terra on her own once again.

7 SUNDAY

Terra pulled into the parking lot of the radio station. She fixed her hair, tucking the loose strands behind her ears before checking her make up in the vanity mirror. Satisfied everything was in order she opened the door of her mustang and slid out from behind the wheel.

She smoothed down the hem of her dress before striding across the lot to the door. Terra yanked open the glass door in temper and moved inside the station.

"Good evening Miss Gallagher, and where's your friend tonight," the man at the security desk asked.

"Gone."

"Did you want me to call the authorities and arrange for…"

"That's not necessary, I doubt Prince Charming will be coming down from his tower any time soon," Terra muttered before moving past the desk in the direction of the booth.

She moved around the room gathering the needed materials for the show as the Wildman wrapped up his time slot. She pulled out a track for her song for the city and then took a seat behind her mike.

"Well, Kauai we're just a few minutes away from the eight-o-clock hour I've got time for one more song before your favorite Lady of the Night takes the mike and opens the request line for you. Aloha, listeners until tomorrow."

Terra watched as Rick switched off his mike and hit the play button for his last song choice of the hour. As she loaded her first set her hands trembled.

"Hey, Terra are you okay?"

"Yeah, just nervous."

"Did you want me to stay?"

"No, I'll be fine; I don't want this guy ta know he's gettin to mi."

"Okay, if you're sure, but just know we're all here if you need us."

"Thanks," Terra said grateful as the song came to a close.

Terra put on her headphones and flipped on the mike.

"Aloha, Kauai the time is now eight o-clock it's time for the magic to start with your own Lady of the Night. I've slipped off my dancing shoes and am ready to kick this party off. So call in your requests and I'll do my best to play them before the witching hour. For now I'm sending out my dedication tonight to a special someone you know who you are this is our final farewell." Terra switched off her mike and pressed play on the song. (*Johnny Hates Jazz 'Shattered Dreams'*) If Kieran had any doubts about Vince's leaving this would silence them. Now all she had to do was wait for his call.

Terra watched the ticking clock unable to look away it was only minutes till midnight and there had been no contact from Kieran. It had been an uneventful night for the show in general, the most memorable call she'd received had come in off the air a request from Lord Night to his Lady (*Crawling Back to You by: Backstreet Boys*). She'd laughed at the dedication but it had helped to easy her nerves knowing that though she didn't see him Vince was still out there watching, listening, and waiting. She wasn't alone.

As she wrapped up the final request for the night she wondered if Vince was right and Kieran had sensed the trap. Terra sighed, it didn't matter if not tonight then soon he would make his move. She slipped the headphones from her ears and rose to her feet. Gathering her things Terra prepared to leave.

Moving down the hall she gave a distracted greeting to security before saying farewell to the receptionist at the desk. Terra stepped outside and crossed the lot to her car. Getting behind the wheel she tossed her things in the passenger seat and sped off into the night for home. As she drove across town the unsettling feeling of being watched set on her again and she craned her neck in an effort to relax.

"So he is still out there?" she muttered. "Come and get mi ya bastard," she hissed as she pulled into the lot outside her hotel.

She mounted the steps and walked into the lobby. Key in hand she stepped on the elevator. The ride up was short and when the door dinged to let her know it was stopping she jumped, her nerves on edge. The waiting was driving her crazy. Stepping out of the car Terra moved down the hall and after sticking the card in the door stepped inside her room.

She'd switched her space to one less secure from Vince's room leaving the blinds open so her stalker could see her, but tonight she chose to stay hidden. Toeing off her shoes in the dark and not bothering with the light, she made her way across the dark room setting her purse down by the bed before grabbing her night clothes.

Terra shed her blouse, unhooked her bra and shrugged it off. She picked up her night shirt to pull it on when her cell phone began to ring. Bending over she pulled it out of her purse and pressed the button to connect the call, before putting it on speaker.

"Hello?" She questioned as she stood up right and moved again to put on her sleep shirt.

"Times up Terra mi luv, mi *Snow White Queen*," Kieran murmured before the line broke signaling he'd hung up.

Terra froze as the *Evanesce* song began to play. Her hands shook at the reality he was there in the room somewhere watching her even now. She pulled on her top and fought for calm as she pulled on her yoga pants under her skirt. Terra crossed to her night table to retrieve the gun she'd left hidden there only to find it gone.

"I trained ya darlin. Did ya really think I wasn't goin ta know where ta look for your gun?" Kieran questioned as he laid his hand upon hers.

Terra flinched moving free of his grasp. "Ya need ta go Kieran I'm not your girl; I never was," Terra said vehemently.

Kieran grabbed her by the wrist and drew her towards him. "Ah but you're wrong lass, you've been mine since the day I took ya in." He stated as he brushed her hair away from her face.

"Ya were like mi da Kieran..." She began in rebuttal.

"Did ya think I groomed ya ta only stand by and watch while another lad bedded ya. No Terra-Ann, I was preparing ya for mi," he corrected as he produced her gun brushing it against her cheek in a twisted caress.

"I never wanted ya that way Kieran."

"Do ya know how disappointed I was when I found out ya'd given yourself ta your Mr. Fenton? I didn't want ta hurt ya lass but ya had to be punished for your betrayal and for lettin that spy in our midst."

"Ya nearly killed mi," Terra snapped in outrage.

"Aye that I did. Took it too far I did, but ya stir mi passions so. Do ya remember our first time?" he asked as he ran the barrel of her gun down the side of her neck.

"It wasn't romantic Kieran; ya raped mi," she reminded as she fought for control of the fear trying to wake in her. The gun he held was loaded and she was not about to provoke him.

"Ya were the best I've ever had luv. I've dreamed of ya ever since. All that pretty skin, the taste of ya, and the feel."

"Kieran please..."

"I've waited a long time for this Terra-Anne," he breathed as the cold barrel of the gun sank into her cleavage.

"I'll never accept this," Terra hissed as goose bumps rose on her flesh and her stomach began to churn with a remembered illness.

"Shh, hush now baby, I'll make it good for ya this time," he vowed before he drew her face to his and kissed her with an intensity that bruised her lips. Teeth pulled at the soft flesh until they drew blood when she cried out in pain he pressed further his tongue delving deep.

Terra retaliated biting him and he roared in rage striking her with the gun. She saw stars and stumbled back away from him.

"Ah, damn ya Terra ya icy bitch why can't ya behave lass. Do ya enjoy pain with your pleasure then?" He hissed as he closed the distance between them.

"If ya do this Kieran I'll kill ya," she roared as she moved blindly in the direction of the door.

"It's enough Snow White, time for your Prince Charming ta wake ya," he muttered as he grabbed her by the hair and pulled her back toward him. As soon as she was within arm's length he grabbed her by the arm once more. "Pretty Terra now you're mine again," he murmured as he pulled her against him so that she felt the proof of his desire pressed against her hip as his arm wrapped about her waist.

"Let her go," Vince demanded as he entered the room his gun trained on the assassin.

"Ah, Mr. Fenton I wondered if ya might turn up?"

"I said release her," Vince commanded again.

"Ya might want ta be careful there yank, ya don't want mi ta hurt your pretty whore," Kieran hissed as he pressed the barrel of her gun to her temple.

"Watch it Kieran that's my wife you're talking about."

"Aye, yank I know. Made mi right mad ta learn I'd trusted ya ta be enough for her, only ta learn ya'd lied to her and us. Went against mi better judgment I'd always meant ta keep her for mi wife."

"She was like your daughter how could you do this to her. She loved you."

"Aye but not enough, she betrayed mi."

"You gave us your blessing."

"And ya left her. Left mi to pick up the pieces. But I couldn't;; she wilted."

"What do ya mean?" Terra asked.

"Nothin mattered ta ya Terra-Anne. Careless ya were lass; like ya wanted someone ta end ya. Ya left the door unlocked for mi then."

Terra blinked startled by the revelation and tried to recall that time; had she been that depressed that she'd invited death?

"Made it right easy for mi ta settle things. I'd hoped that after ya'd had your taste of death that we'd be able ta move on but ya locked mi away."

"Ya nearly killed mi."

"Aye because it was what ya thought ya wanted. When ya vanished I thought ta let ya go but I could never forget ya lass. Always wanted ya back where ya belonged by mi side. When we started this little game I thought we'd finally come full circle that at last ya were ready ta accept mi again that we could be together."

"I never..."

"Hush girl, I ain't finished. Things were goin well I thought, until he had ta go and turn up again. Ya had no right ta touch her Mr. Fenton." Kieran said with outrage.

"I had every right she's my wife."

"Was your wife yank; ya gave up that right when ya abandoned her and us for your job. I warned ya ta leave; you'd have been wise ta do so."

"Did you really think I'd leave her again for you to hurt?" Vince questioned with disgust.

"I did ya. Always took ya for a nave and a cur."

"I never lied about how I felt about Terra, never used her to..."

"Ya lied about everything Mr. Fenton, if ya'd loved her as ya claimed you'd have known the danger ya left her in. Would have protected her as I did."

"Protected her! You nearly killed her!" Vince shouted in fury.

"I protected her from the others. They wanted her dead. I convinced them ta let me handle her punishment. Do ya think I wanted ta hurt her that way? Better mi than them." Kieran hissed.

"Why do this?" Terra asked trying to sort through his madness.

"Because I made ya Terra-Anne and I won't let another have ya again. I love ya lass I'm the only one who can, "he whispered. The barrel of his gun moved down her cheek as his hand around her waist caressed her abdomen with suggestion of what he still wished of her. He was careful to keep her between him and Vince's gun.

"You knew I'd be here, how?" Vince asked.

"Ya put on a good act last night believable but Terra despite her dedication earlier didn't look like a woman abandoned." Kieran answered.

"Let mi go Kieran."

"Never, ya belong ta mi, mi, little Snow White and I won't give ya up again. If I can't have ya no one will," he vowed.

"I'm not your little Snow White any more Kieran," Terra snapped in defiance as she stomped on the instep of his foot. She threw an elbow back into his solar-plexus. He recoiled in instinct to protect himself and when he no longer held her she kicked him in the nuts dropping him to the floor like a stone.

Her gun fell from powerless fingers and she picked it up. With an efficiency born from years of training she screwed the silencer into place on the end of the gun and turned the weapon that had been pointed at her to his temple. "I haven't been since ya put your hands on mi," she said her voice cold as ice. Terra squeezed the trigger the soft sound of a pop interrupted the next line of the song as the smell of gun powder hit her senses. She watched as her mentor fell to the floor in a heap eyes unseeing blood flowing from his head.

Terra was aware she'd be covered in the man's blood but she was unaware of it on her skin; only the metallic smell of copper gave hint to the mess she'd made. Her gun fell from shaking hands as she blinked trying to chase out the fear and disgust that threatened to drive her mad.

His words were a twisted and terrifying mass that writhed in her mind like a nest of vipers. Though he no longer clung to her she could still feel his covetous arms wrapped about her like a nightmare that she was unable to wake from. She wanted to scream but her throat was dry and raw, her lips cracked and bloody, refused to part to emit the sound.

Terra rubbed her hand over her face wiping away tears and blood smearing both.

"Terra..."

She blinked her green eyes lifting from the dead man to her husband. His blue eyes studied her filled with concern.

"I had to do it," she muttered.

Vince nodded, letting her know he understood though why he hadn't been allowed to, baffled him, he'd wanted to. For what the assassin had done to her, he'd wanted nothing more than to kill the bastard with his bare hands.

"If I'd not done it he'd have haunted me forever," Terra whispered.

✦ ✦ ✦

Vince moved to her side and drew her into the shelter of his arms. With care, he led her away from the dead man's side. "Sit down for me Terra," he requested as he stopped in front of the chair. She did so without a word and he walked into the bathroom, grabbing a rag he wet it. After ringing it out he returned to his wife's side and with care cleaned up her face. He then took out his phone and punched in the number for his agency contact for a cleanup crew.

"Come on love, let's get out of here," he whispered.

"I can't go with ya, not after this your employer..."

"Is looking for Intel on Kieran and his employer; you have both. We can trade it for your freedom."

"But I just..."

"Eliminated a threat to your welfare; he'd have kept coming...my employers will understand," Vince stated.

"If they don't?"

"Then' we'll leave together. I won't leave you again, Terra."

"Thank you."

"Come on lets go home," he said again and he held out his hand for her. Terra got to her feet and took it in her own. Together they walked out; leaving the grisly scene behind them.

PART 2

Darkness Stirs

8 Unknown

Zaharrah walked through the double doors of the old library; passed the common section to the area designated for employees only. She was exhausted from the grueling work in Ithaca and disgusted to have been cheated out of the credit for the find. After all, she'd only managed to recover and restore one of the more valuable artifacts, the signet ring of Odysseus, and the snake, Dr. Ian Broody had claimed every part of the dig for himself.

Zaharrah smiled as she recalled that Ian had gotten his in the end. The lovely Annalynn Darcy Gallagher had thrown his ring in his face and told him to take a walk. Zaharrah had been impressed by the display. When they met Dr. Gallagher had seemed so timid, that the anger she'd displayed at the man's betrayal had been more than Zaharrah expected from the woman.

As she moved down the hall her path crossed a dark haired man with eyes the color of cold steel.

"Zaharrah, I didn't think you'd be back so soon," he said surprised by the sight of her.

"Magnus, the dig site on the isle is contained, the true ring hidden. I'm here to check in before I head home, and you?"

"I'm leaving the order," Magnus whispered.

"What? Why?" Zaharrah asked alarmed. Magnus was one of their best agents. Losing him would be a grave loss.

"There's nothing left to keep me here," he replied, with a cool shrug.

"I thought you believed in the cause," Zaharrah stated confusion in her brown eyes.

"I never believed in their war."

"Then, why didn't you leave sooner?"

"I stayed for you Zaharrah," he murmured as he brushed a stray lock of her dark hair away from her face. "I had hoped..." he began with regret as he played with the errant strand, running it between his fingers, enjoying the feel of it against his skin.

"Magnus, please, you know I'm married," she muttered with discomfort as she stepped away from his touch.

"An Outsider," he snapped with disgust. "It should have been me. I'd have cared for you, protected you..." he said moving closer to her. His large frame dwarfing her 5'9 figure, making her feel uneasy and overly aware of his power here. If he wanted to Magnus was more than capable of snapping her in two and she'd be powerless to stop him.

"I never saw you that way," she stated calmly; refusing to let him intimidate her.

"I know. I thought with time maybe..." he sighed letting the thought trail off before backing away from her, respecting her space and her choice. "But you fell for the Mossad agent instead," he said with a shrug that gave the impression he didn't care but she knew better. She'd hurt him when he found out through the council rather than her. "Now, I'm getting out. I can't watch you with him, but more than that I won't give my life for their lie."

"What does that mean?" Zaharrah asked curious.

"The elders have been lying to us all. There are things about our missions; they keep hidden. You should consider getting out as well," Magnus suggested before he moved on, back the way she'd come.

Zaharrah sighed before she started back down the hall. As she reached the meeting room Magnus's words circled round in her head and she wondered what he'd learned to leave him so disenchanted with the cause.

9 Jerusalem, Israel

Zaharrah stepped through the front door of the home she shared with Gunnar Dayan and dropped her bag on the floor. She slipped off her work boots before starting across the living room. Her brown eyes lit with joy at the sight of the tanned muscular man with green eyes and dark hair. He crossed the distance between them in two strides and wrapped his arms around her.

"Welcome home beautiful," he murmured before he tilted his head down to capture her lips in a hungry kiss. He drank deeply from them, his fingers sinking into her dark hair, breaking up her natural curls.

"I missed you Gunnar," she whispered as she wrapped her arms around his neck.

"As did I," he assured her before placing a kiss on her forehead, followed by her cheek. "How was your trip?"

"We'll talk about it after," she promised before she drew his mouth back to her own. Her kiss was wild and desperate. It had been too long since she held him so. Gunnar had no objection to her reply. He swept his young wife into his arms and carried her into their bedroom.

He lay her down on their bed and peeled her out of her clothes thrilling at the ability to touch her once more.

Zaharrah lost herself in Gunnar's touch but soon his hands and even his mouth on her heated flesh wasn't enough. She helped him to undress and after reveling in the feel of his body under her fingers, she drew him inside her and rode out the storm of emotion that followed as the young couple made love.

10

Gunnar kissed Zaharrah's neck as he lay beside her in the bed. "How was the trip?" he asked again.

"Okay. I got the job done, but Dr. Broody stole all the credit."

"I'm sorry, my love."

"No big deal. There will be other digs, but not with him."

"I guess not. I'm glad you got to come home early though," he whispered as he brushed his fingers over her naked belly.

"Yeah, so am I. This was a great welcome home. I'm glad you were here."

"Me too. I'm hoping for a second round after a meal," he whispered suggestively as he ran his finger between her breasts.

"I think that's doable," she assured him before she slipped out of the bed and pulled on his shirt. Gunnar pulled on his pants and followed her into the kitchen.

Zaharrah opened the fridge and eyed its contents with interest. She shook her head with disbelief. There wasn't much there.

"What have you been eating while I was away?"

"What I could find," he answered with a guilty shrug.

Zaharrah chuckled as she pulled out some fresh fruit and eggs. It wasn't much but it would do for now. Turning from the fridge she pulled out a skillet, a knife and a bowl. Then with a skill honed from years of practice, she cut up the fruit preparing it; before turning her focus to the eggs.

As she began to fry a couple, Gunnar moved behind her, he slid up against her back, wrapped his arms around her waist. His hands slid under his shirt to stir her with the need that, watching her work, had awoken within him.

"Gunnar if you keep that up I'll burn the eggs," she warned with amusement.

"We have more," he whispered before he kissed the side of her neck.

"I thought you were hungry?" Zaharrah laughed.

"I was, but there is just something about seeing you in nothing but my shirt working in here that makes me crazy," he murmured before nipping her ear.

Zaharrah sighed under his ministrations, her eyes falling shut reveling in the feel of him. She figured the eggs were a lost cause but she didn't care. She'd been away from him too long.

"I want my shirt back Zaharrah, take it off," he requested.

"I'm not cooking for you naked Gunnar," she breathed. She bit her lip as his teasing caress grew more insistent and stretched under his touch seeking more. Gunnar would persuade her into doing as he asked and she loved his methods.

The quiet moment was shattered by the shrill cry of his cell phone.

"Forgive me," he requested before he let her go to answer the offending object.

"Hello."

Zaharrah watched as he listened to the other side of the conversation.

"Speaking."

She blinked and watched as all that playful heat from moments ago faded, the hard gleam of the warrior was in his eyes.

"Understood. Yes sir, about an hour sir," Gunnar stated. "Thank you sir, I won't be late," he assured the person on the other end before disconnecting the call.

"Trouble?"

"Some. I shouldn't be gone long."

"Did you still want your food?"

"I've got some time yet," he assured her as he tucked his phone back in his pants.

"I heard an hour."

"No, CO gave me two. He's aware your back," Gunnar said with a smile before he drew her back against him. Zaharrah switched off the stove

"Thank him for me," she requested before she turned and embraced him.

"I will," he assured her. "Zaharrah, if I'm away and you're ever in trouble, I want you to call my friend Sam."

"Sam?"

"Sam Abrams. He's an American. I'll program the number in your phone. He's a good man I trust him..." he began before Zaharrah kissed him; ending his train of thought again.

"Okay...I understand," she assured him.

"Good," he replied.

"Anything else we need to discuss?" she questioned.

"No," he assured her.

"Good, let's not waist anymore time," she whispered before she kissed him.

11

Zaharrah watched as Gunnar left for his meet with his superior, she hated that he was going but she understood why. He was a soldier; same as her. She'd chosen a difficult path but she knew it was the right one. Gunnar loved her and she him.

But as she watched him go something Magnus said stirred in her mind. She'd felt something in Ithaca. A shadow and a threat, some unseen danger that lurked. She wondered now what it was and if it were possible that Magnus was right and the elders were hiding things from them.

For as long as she could remember she and her people had been moving in secret to keep certain things from being discovered, but why? She'd never been made aware of the reason. She did as she was told because it was how she'd been raised. You never question orders and she never had until Gunnar. She'd defied council law when she married him in secret. She'd been careful to keep him hidden but they'd been discovered somehow.

When the truth came out she'd had to make promises that didn't sit well with her. Things she'd yet to tell Gunnar.

She blinked as she wondered for the first time if her loyalty to the order was misplaced. If Magnus was questioning it, then maybe she should be also. Picking up her phone; she pushed the number on speed dial that would put her in touch with him.

"Hello?"

"Can we meet?" She asked.

"Sure."

"The usual spot in ten minutes," Zaharrah muttered.

"I'll be waiting," he assured her before ending the call.

Zaharrah put away her phone, grabbed her purse and pulled on her shoes before stepping out the door.

12

Zaharrah stepped into the dim lit bar her brown eyes skimmed the faces in the crowd. She spotted Magnus at a table in the back alone his steel gray eyes watching the patrons and the doors.

She crossed the floor and took the empty seat across from him.

"Zaharrah nice to see you again so soon, though I figured you'd be with him."

"He got called out."

"I see. So, what can I do for you my dear?"

"I wanted to ask you about what you said earlier. What sort of things are they hiding and how do you know?"

Magnus smiled. "You know the cave?"

"Of course, we all take duty there occasionally to ensure it remains hidden."

"Do you know why?"

"No. Only that it's dangerous."

"There is a sword there hidden deep in the earth. The sword of a god that killed another. Sealed with it is a spirit."

"What? That's..."

"Crazy, yeah I know. But it's the truth."

"What proof do you have?"

"The archives. I read it among other things in all that text the elders forbid us to see."

"The Archives..."

"I broke in. There's more but that's just a taste. Here's a copy of the piece I'm refereeing to," Magnus offered as he handed over a piece of paper.

Zaharrah took the page and tucked it in her pocket. "Why tell me?"

"Because, despite what's happened, I still care about you. I still want you and I won't let them get you killed protecting their lie," Magnus answered before he took her hand in his and kissed it.

She drew back from his touch and got back to her feet. "I have to go, but thank you."

"Zaharrah, when you're ready, I'll be waiting," he whispered before he picked up his drink and swallowed.

Zaharrah turned and walked out, the paper in her pocket was burning a hole in her mind and her gut. If what Magnus was telling her was the truth, then there was a lot more going on than anyone knew.

As she got back in her car, she flipped on the light and pulled out the page. Her brown eyes skimmed over the text and she cursed. It seemed a trip to the archives was in order.

13 Unknown

Zaharrah slipped into the library that housed the secret base of the order of the Black Hand. She moved through the passages into the corridor for the members. As she crept down the dark hall toward the section labeled council chambers.

She'd seen the door many times over the years. In her youth she'd wondered what was within, as an adult she'd dismissed it as unimportant; until tonight. As she approached the door, she took out the copy of her grandfather's key, she'd made in her youth.

Zaharrah had never been brave enough to use it. She'd understood if she were caught the punishment would be severe but fear couldn't hold her out tonight. She fit the key in the lock and slipped inside.

The room was dark and smelled like ancient scrolls. She lit a candle near the door and moved deeper into the room. Even with the dim lighting she found the scroll Magnus had copied easily. There were clear signs it had been disturbed recently if one knew what to look for, yet no signs of damage. As she got near it the scroll pulsed with the same menacing feel she'd experienced in Ithaca.

Reading it she cursed as she found that what Magnus had given her earlier was indeed real. A part of her had wanted it to be a trick of some kind. Zaharrah felt her stomach roll with illness as she wondered for the first time who or what the order served? What was their end game in all this? As she read other scrolls she was certain of one thing: the vow she made to be with Gunnar she had to break it.

14

Zaharrah slipped back into her apartment as the sun began to rise. She put her bag down on the floor and secured the door. With care she hid the satchel she'd brought back and its pilfered contents for the night. It would have to be moved in the morning to a more secure location but for now the spot in her home would have to do.

If she was going to get clear of the order she'd need leverage. The best thing she'd been able to think of was a portion of the secrets they were hiding.

When the bag was secure, Zaharrah sank down into bed. She was just beginning to dose off when Gunnar crept into the room.

"Everything okay?" she asked pleased he was back.

"Yeah, I've got a mission coming up soon but for now I'm clear," he assured her before he drew her into his arms. "What are you still doing up?"

"I couldn't sleep."

"Something wrong?"

"No, I'm fine, just the time change," she assured him.

"The worst part of travel," he muttered with understanding before he kissed her back.

"Yeah, but it's worth it if it brings me back to this," she whispered before snuggling closer.

"I couldn't agree more," he murmured before closing his eyes.

Zaharrah enjoyed the feel of Gunnar wrapped around her and tried not to worry about the order and what they would do.

15

Zaharrah walked near the Scottish lake a strange mist rolled over the countryside making it hard to see the rocky hills beyond. She followed the used path that she'd know blind, through the fog, straight to the cavern she'd protected loyally in her youth.

Without hesitation she walked inside wondering where the guard was. As she made her way down the dark passage she noted fresh tracks and cursed. Someone else was there. Urgency pressed upon her and the casual walk became a desperate run.

As she reached the end of the tunnel a man with his back to her wrapped his hands around the grip of the sword.

"Don't!" She shouted in warning but her words came too late. The sword was drawn. The spirit it held prisoner was set free. Zaharrah felt a rush of power tear through the darkness. Fear woke within her. She blinked as the torches within burst to life and when her eyes opened she was no longer in the cave.

Stony earth was suddenly lightly packed earth. She could see olive trees in the distance and the smell of the sea hung in the air. Ithaca. She wondered how she'd gotten there as she walked in the direction of the cave of nymphs where the dig was still under way.

She saw Broody and the team working on the cataloging work and noted that Broody guarded the whip closely. It was what held him now, not the ring that had been stolen which the order had her replace and return.

The sword and the whip were one and the same, she'd need to watch both. As she thought it, the cave and the sight faded from her mind and she found she stood out in the desert overlooking the Dead Sea. She wondered at the reason as she'd not seen anything in her reading to connect it to the rest but before she could look further the scene changed again and she was home aware that one of the gods was watching, waiting.

She felt pursued and aware that not just her life but those around her as well were in danger. A sense of dread filled her as she realized that if she stayed where she was then she was marking Gunnar for death.

She gasped in pain as the fear that had begun to stir inside her, swallowed her whole. Her mind fell deep into the blackest darkness she'd ever known. In it she felt the icy touch of the spirit that stirred against her.

"I will have you for my own," it hissed before it tormented her further with the promise of the things it would bring against her if she continued down her current path.

16

Zaharrah woke in a cold sweat, a silent scream tore from her throat as the nightmare ended. She looked at Gunnar beside her and tears wet her cheeks at the sight of him alive and whole. She wanted to kiss him to touch him to assure herself he was real but as she moved to do so a flash of the dream surfaced in her mind and stayed her hand.

She saw her family gathered round a table with her and Gunnar and their children as she longed for their acceptance of him. Everyone she cared about under one roof celebrating then a dark clad figure entered the room unannounced and eyed the gathering with hatred. He stretched out his hand and with some unseen weapon began to inflict pain upon each one seated tormenting them.

"Stop this! You have no rights here," Zaharrah shouted with outrage.

"I have every right. I warned you that I would come for you. I told you if you didn't let them go that they would suffer at my hand. Now they pay for your greed. His children should never have been they were meant to be mine," the figure muttered with rage and she watched with disbelief as he touched her son and daughter and they fell over dead.

"No! Stop this!"

"It will all end if you come with me now," the shadow promised.

Zaharrah blinked and the image faded she drew a breath, only a dream, she assured herself as she reached for Gunnar again. Instantly the image before her shifted. She saw Gunnar not as he was, sleeping peacefully and untouched but broken, bleeding, begging for death; while the spirit that sought her laughed and waited for her surrender.

"His suffering will never end until you say yes to me," the voice hissed in her mind.

"I will never embrace you," she shouted in defiance as she lashed out at the dark figure; trying to fight him for hurting her love. But she was powerless against him. All her efforts to inflict harm proved fruitless and without effect. She could do nothing but watch Gunnar suffer.

"Let him go," Zaharrah demanded.

"No you let him go. Will you see him suffer, die even, because you refuse to walk away from him."

"You have no right to do this! I am his." Zaharrah raged.

The image faded the memory slipping into the dark recesses of her mind. She looked once more at Gunnar and swallowed back a sob. Such horrible dreams, why? What was happening to her? She wondered as she drew back from her sleeping spouse.

"NO! YOU ARE MINE! YOU ALWAYS HAVE BEEN AND YOU ALWYS WILL BE. YOU WERE PROMISED TO ME THE DAY YOU WERE BORN!" The voice in her mind roared back in rage now that she was once more in reality. She choked back a scream as she felt the icy hands of the spirit wrap around her shoulders.

It wasn't just dream. Her tormentor was real as were his threats. If she didn't leave them everyone she cared for all that she loved... She couldn't let that happen, not to Gunnar, not to anyone near her. Whatever was holding on to her now and whatever form he was coming for her in later down the road, when it found her she would be damn sure it found no one with her.

Slipping from the bed Zaharrah dressed in the dark and then made her way out of the bedroom. She crossed the floor to the kitchen and scribbled a quick note for Gunnar before grabbing her satchel from the night before. She then crept out of the apartment she called home.

As she moved down the crowded street she paused for only a moment to look back with regret and a heavy heart at her home and the man she was leaving behind.

"Good bye my love," she whispered before turning away once more. She took a few more steps away from her life and then vanished into the crowd without a trace.

PART 3

DISCOVERIES

17 DEAD SEA
APRIL
WEDNESDAY
5AM

Sunlight spilled over the rocky desert terrain near the Dead Sea. A short distance from the water's edge construction had already begun. The foundation of the UN Embassy building had been poured. Half the frame was already raised. By week's end the basic work would be complete and the real construction would begin. As the workers began to arrive to begin the new day they groaned at the sight of the gathered protesters waiting at the property line. They held various signs with numerous slogans arguing against the UN Embassy sight.

The Foreman cursed. When would these people give it up? They'd been on site every day from dawn until dusk. All there picketing and grumbling were in vain. The site was approved there was no evidence of historical relics in the area chosen. Building would continue.

"All right boys let's back them up," the foreman stated before moving on to inspect the work from the day before. So far there were no signs of sabotage, he hoped that remained true.

Ben Cooper watched as his men herded the protesters back out of harm's way, before turning his full attention to the blue prints. Studying the drawing, the sound of the crowd faded to the background it was just another day on the site.

"Stop right there!" a lone voice rose above the din. The foreman recognized it as his head of security. Someone had decided to push their luck he mused. It happened at least once a day. It was a part of the norm here; any minute the offender would apologize and melt back into the crowd. Ben waited for the response but none came instead a second warning was given. "Freeze or you will be fired upon!"

Ben glanced up from the building plans in the direction of the confrontation. He watched with fascination and mild disgust as the intruder kept coming. Their security agent opened fire. The sound of the gun silenced the protesters and sent some running for cover. The foreman looked on as the intruder fell to the dusty earth, blood flowing from his chest. This was no ordinary day. It was the first time anyone had been hurt, he hoped it would be the last.

Ben watched as the security agent moved in to check the body. He kicked something out of the man's hand then knelt to check for a pulse. The foreman looked on with disbelief as the security agent scrambled back from the body turned and ran.

"Run!" The frantic cry filled the silence the gun shots had created. Ben Cooper looked on as the people around him scurried like ants. The order registered in his mind and he turned and fled away from the construction site for some kind of cover.

The ground beneath his feet trembled as an explosion rocked the earth. From the cover of his truck Ben looked back at the site. A crater lay in the earth where the intruder had fallen. The earth around it was scorched. The timber for the embassy building frame burned, pieces snapped like twigs. The foundation was cracked and Mr. Cooper cursed.

A week's worth of work had been undone in an instant. "Is everyone okay?" He shouted checking on his men. They nodded and some muttered replies. Ben breathed a sigh of relief. No one was hurt. The bomber had been taken down early enough for everyone to get clear. "Let's get this fire out and assess the damage."

The work crew began the task of recovery as security moved in to investigate the crater. Mr. Cooper was discussing how to begin repairing the site when he got a page.

"This had better be important."

"Sir, it's about the crater we found something here that you're going to have to notify the boss of."

"What is it?"

"We're not sure. You best come have a look."

"I'm on my way." Ben said with impatience. He then turned his attention to his crew. "We'll finish this in a bit there's some kind of problem at the crater." The foreman stated and he turned from the site in the direction of the security team.

As he approached the crater he spotted the problem. Sticking out of the debris was the mouth of an earthen vase. "Damn," he grumbled knowing the ramifications of the discovery. If it was from the ground here as it appeared then it was an artifact and no further work could be done. If it was not native to this ground then it was an elaborate hoax. Either way no more work would be done that day. Ben pulled out his phone and punched in the number for their boss.

"Tell the team to stop what they're doing," he snapped at security. The phone on the other end rang and as he waited for someone to answer he cursed again. It was shaping up to be a shitty morning.

18

We have a problem." Russell York stated flustered as he walked into the office of his superior.

"What is it?"

"I just spoke to the foreman on our project near the Dead Sea. Seems there was a bombing attempt; no one was injured but they've unearthed some sort of artifact out there."

"I thought we surveyed the land and found nothing," Mr. Halden said with irritation.

"We did sir but until we verify it's nothing all labor has to stop."

"Get a team in there with no biases and get that thing out of my build site."

"If it turns out to be an artifact sir?"

"Then we'll cross that bridge when we get to it."

"Who do you want to handle this matter?"

"Get me Dr. Ian Broody. We've used him before. Once I know what we're dealing with he can elect any additional team members he may need."

"Very good sir, consider it done." Russell turned and walked back into his own office.

19

Ian Broody stood in front of his floor length mirror on the inside face of his closet door. He ran a comb through his damp, clean cut, salt and pepper hair, smoothing out the ends. He turned his steel gray gaze to the crimson tie hanging loose around his neck. Straightened it and made it tight. Ian then pulled a black vest from a hanger and drew it on over a crisp, wrinkle free white dress shirt. He was securing the buttons when his phone rang.

Ian turned from his reflection and crossed the pristine white Berber carpet to his white oak dresser. He picked up the offending object and noting the number swore before pressing the button to connect the call. Not one to lose time he pressed the button to switch the call to speaker then turned his attention back to the mirror.

"Hello Mr. York."

"Dr. Broody. I'm glad I caught you in."

"What is it I can do for you Russell?" Ian questioned, he didn't have a lot of time to waste. He felt it better to skip the pleasantries and get right to it. As he waited for an answer he finished buttoning his vest.

"We found an artifact of some sort at our newest project site and we need your expertise to determine its validity."

"What kind of artifact – where?" Ian asked with interest. He pulled on his suit jacket and tucked a red silk handkerchief in his pocket.

"A vase. Near the Dead Sea."

"There are other archeologists in your area more qualified…"

"I'm sure there are. You can bring them in if the need arises. He asked for you. We need this kept quiet."

"I can't leave until after the benefit. I'll expect triple my usual fee."

"You'll get it. We need this one solved ASAP."

"Fine, I'll be on the first flight out after the benefit," Ian assured him.

"Good, we'll be expecting you. You're reservation will be at the King David Hotel. All expenses will be covered as usual.

"Thank you."

"No, Dr. Broody, thank you." Russell said before he disconnected the call.

Ian made a few adjustments to his appearance and picked up his phone. He noted the time. Gathered his things then packed his travel bag so that he could go straight from the benefit to the airport. He booked a red eye over to Tel Aviv and then left for the Smithsonian.

20 TEL AVIV APRIL THURSDAY 12PM

Ian Broody passed through customs, then headed out of the airport. When he stepped into the heat of the noonday sun, he was pleased to find a car waiting for him. Ian tossed his bag in the trunk and slid into the backseat. Once the door was closed the car pulled away from the curb. It set off into traffic headed toward Jerusalem.

Ian yawned. It had been a prolonged flight over. He'd gotten little, to no, sleep. He was looking forward to a good long rest at the hotel. Ian was in the process of planning his activities before bed when he glanced out the window. He swore seeing they were headed out of Jerusalem and further east.

"Driver, where are we going?"

"Straight to the site, Mr. York's orders."

"Damn, so much for a nap," Ian grumbled. He threw out any notions of an extended period of rest or relaxation. They would have to wait until after he saw the artifact. For now he'd have to settle with what little he could snag en route. Ian closed his eyes and hoped the trip over would be a slow one.

The car slowed as it drew near the Dead Sea. Ian opened his eyes and peered out the window. He noted a burned up construction site in the distance. Ian wondered for a moment what they had been building there, then reminded himself it was best not to get too concerned with Mr. York's business. The car came to a stop in front of a white tent. Ian stepped out into the heat and sighed; it felt worse now and the air was thick with salt. It was the sort of place a man could, without warning, vanish from without a trace. He was grateful that he'd managed to avoid Russell's bad side.

"Your things will be waiting for you at the hotel. Good luck Dr. Broody," the driver stated.

Ian flinched the comment having startled him. He'd forgotten the other man. "Thank you," He muttered before he slammed the car door. Ian walked the short distance to the tent entrance and stepped inside.

"Doctor, so good to see you again," Russell greeted. His lips held a smile that didn't reach his green eyes.

Broody felt his palms sweat. Mr. York was not happy about the artifact and that meant his boss wasn't either. "Russell I wasn't expecting to see you here."

"I trust your flight over was a good one?"

"Yes, I had hoped to rest…"

"Of course, you must be exhausted." Russell York said with sympathy. He straightened out his black tie. Ian marveled at the man's ability to wear a full suit and not sweat. It was as if the heat couldn't touch him. "Forgive me for keeping you. We'll get you on to the hotel just as soon as you've had a look at our vase."

"Where is it?" Ian asked hoping to get the initial consultation over with fast.

"Follow me," Mr. York replied and he led Ian towards the back of the tent.

Ian came to the edge of a small crater. He noted the edges were charred. "What happened here?" he murmured recalling the burned construction site.

"Suicide bomb."

Ian swallowed, he hadn't really expected an answer. He reasoned that he must be standing on the blast spot and fought the urge to wretch. "Why?"

"That is not your concern Dr. Broody. The vase is just inside the crater."

Ian nodded and turned his focus inside the hole. He spotted the lip of a vase sticking out of the shifted sand. Ian set down his travel bag and pulled out his tool kit. He then stepped into the crater. With care and precision he began the task of unearthing the artifact.

21 DEAD SEA
APRIL
THURSDAY
8PM

Ian Broody stared in disbelief at the uncovered vase. It was made of red clay and formed in the style of the people of the area in 18th 19th century B.C. Yet the image depicted on the clay was not. In black on the earthen vase was a familiar Grecian icon. In it Zeus sat upon his throne high atop Mount Olympus gazing down upon man. A crown was upon his head. In his right hand he held the lightning bolt of his authority; poised waiting to strike.

"Well?" Russell questioned a hint of irritation in his voice.

Ian jumped startled, he'd forgotten the other man in his work. "I'm not sure yet. I need equipment for dating it and a team of experts. This is either a hoax or an unusual find of great significance."

"Who do you want?" Mr. York asked.

"Dr. Omar Bashir from Israel's archeology department; Dr. Fahim Manal from Jordan, Dr. Hakeem Kadin from Egypt and Dr. Annalynn Darcy Gallagher from the Smithsonian."

"Why Gallagher? She almost caused us a lot of trouble in Ithaca."

"She's thorough for one. Maybe the best when it comes to details, better than most at any rate. She's also completely unbiased by religious leaning. Anna's a truth seeker."

"Fine, gather your team. I'll get your equipment. I need this sorted out and quick."

"I will. We'll get this vase out of the ground tomorrow and have it dated by week's end. While we wait for the results we'll go over every intricate detail."

"Thank you Ian, I'm sure this will be in the best hands possible," Mr. York said with a smile. Ian stood up. He took one last look at the vase before climbing out of the crater. As he reached Russell's side the man grabbed him by the arm, stopping his progress. "But Ian understand that if Miss Gallagher gets out of hand I'll deal with her and hold you responsible."

"Got it. I'll make sure she's on a short leash and her mouth stays shut."

"Good. Now, go back to the hotel. Make your calls and get some rest."

Ian nodded. Mr. York let him go and he made his way out of the tent into the night air. He drew a breath trying to settle his nerves. Russell was dangerous, he knew it well but he paid well. Ian counted the risk as worthwhile when he considered the profit he'd turned over the years. Besides he enjoyed the unknown and the vase was that and more.

If it was real it would be a real eye opener. Where had it come from? Why had the initial survey of the site missed it? So many questions circled about in his mind. He trusted that his team would help him to solve the mystery. Ian sighed, clearing his head of the various questions; knowing if he let them they'd keep him from sleep. He'd make his calls do what he needed to keep Anna happy and then turn in.

Dr. Broody watched his car pull up in front of him and smiled it was nice to have prompt service. He stepped into the car and took a seat in the back. Once the door was shut he closed his eyes.

22 WASHINGTON DC
APRIL
THURSDAY
10AM

A pair of hazel eyes peered through a lighted magnifying glass studying a clay cup. Anna blinked then brushed a moist cotton swab on the rim of the cup cleaning it. She'd been working on cleaning and restoring the goblet for well over three months now and still had yet to figure it out. It was a less valuable piece from a larger private collection that the Smithsonian had collected from a British noble. It wasn't important and had been moved from the main site to the auction house.

Despite its simplistic appearance Anna felt there was something deceptive about it. For one, it was surprisingly heavy for a simple earthen chalice. She'd placed a request to ultrasound test it but so far no one had responded. Then there were times when the thing felt warm to the touch despite the coolness of her office. There was something more to it than she could see.

Anna shrugged. "What are you?" she murmured, then sighed. Anna rinsed her cleaning tool removing the blackened soil form the cotton tip. Her thoughts ran over clay cups in the area trying to place it. She cursed, when her phone rang interrupting her train of thought. Looking at the ID she groaned before connecting the call.

"Hello Dr. Broody."

"Dr. Gallagher I'm glad I caught you before lunch. I've got a puzzle for you."

"Oh. What kind?" Anna questioned with interest. It burned her, she cared. After what he'd pulled last time they worked together it shouldn't matter to her, but it did. Ian was a credit hog. If he was calling her it must be a good one.

"I found a vase near the Dead Sea. It reflects the style, make of the area for the 18th 19th century B.C. but the image on the vase is Grecian."

"Have you dated it?" Anna asked as she scribbled down notes in the margins of her current repot on the cup.

"Not yet, but it looks authentic."

"You're sure?"

"80%"

"Okay, I'm in. I'll pass my current work onto Phillip and get the next flight out."

"Thank you, Anna."

"You can thank me later Ian. If this turns out to be real I get credit for my contributions for the find. I won't stand for another Ithaca."

"Anna I'm…"

"Save your apologies Ian. We both know you don't mean it. I won't be used by you again to build your career. I want it in writing that if this thing proves to be real I will share in the credit or I'm out."

"You'll have it."

"In that case consider me on my way." Anna murmured. She then disconnected the call. Anna switched off her light and secured the cup in her safe before rolling her chair away from the desk. Getting to her feet she pulled a pencil out from behind her ear. She smoothed out her blonde hair tucking it back in place. Anna turned her head cracking stiff joints in her neck and shoulders then stepped out of her office into the main hall of the staff only portion of the building.

She turned left and headed down the passage until she reached a set of double doors. Anna knocked, as she waited she studied the plaque over the doors, "Dr. Phillip King Director of Antiquities." She hoped Phillip was in a good mood. He wasn't fond of unannounced interruptions. Anna heard a curse from within and winced.

"Oh blast. Who is there?"

"Dr. King, it's me Anna. I'm sorry to interrupt but I just got a call from Dr. Broody…"

"Oh, Anna my dear girl, please do come in. I was just about to come check on your progress with your latest project."

Anna let out a breath she'd been unaware of holding. She opened the door and stepped inside. Phillip sat behind his long oak desk, a stack of paperwork in front of him. His blue eyes looked up and studied her with concern.

"You said Ian called?"

"Yes."

"Are you okay?" Phillip asked, recalling they hadn't been on speaking terms last night.

"I'm fine sir." She assured him.

"Don't suppose he mentioned where he was at? No one has seen or heard from him since the benefit last night," Phillip groused.

"Actually he did. He's got a mystery on his hands near the Dead Sea. He's requested my aid with it."

"Are you going?"

"Yes, he promised me my credit in the find on paper. I was wondering if you can take over the rest of the details on the cup."

"Of course. Are you sure you want to do this?" Philip questioned as he took her hand in his and gave it a gentle squeeze.

Anna smiled; touched that he seemed to care. She wished her parents had been more understanding. "Yes. He owes me and I plan on collecting; besides I could use a trip out of here for a while."

"All right. I'll clear the flight and travel expenses with the museum. Be careful Anna, you're my best student. I don't want to see anything happen to you."

"I will Phillip and thanks."

"You're welcome my dear."

"I'll get that cup and my notes on it for you," Anna said then she turned and left headed back to her office.

She stepped into the cramped corporate room and crossed the blue carpeted floor to her desk. Anna opened her personal safe. Took out the cup and placed it in a satchel. She then secured the safe and gathered her notes. Materials gathered she stepped back out into the hall. She jumped startled to find Phillip waiting outside her door.

"Here you go," she murmured. Anna handed over the satchel and her notes.

"The flight and expenses have been cleared. Take this. It'll cover all your expenses. Good luck Anna."

"Thanks."

"Anna, for what it's worth I'm sorry for what he did to you," Phillip said. He surprised her when he drew her into his arms and hugged her. This sort of emotional display was foreign to her but from Phillip she accepted it returning the fatherly embrace unsure.

"You tried to warn me," Anna said with a shrug.

He let her go before responding. "True, but I'm not one to say I told you so. If I had my way he'd have been cut loose, unfortunately the board voted against me."

"I appreciate the thought but they'd never let their best contributor go over a credit squabble."

"It was more than that dear."

"Yes, I know it but the rest doesn't matter to them."

"It matters to me. Don't let him hurt you again."

"I won't I've learned my lesson," she assured him then turned and left.

23 DEAD SEA
APRIL
FRIDAY
7AM

Anna stepped out of the cab, in the distance lay the Dead Sea, it was crowded with tourists that had both come to swim in the buoyant water and those who sought its unique mud. She stared at the dusty ground mixed with rocky terrain through her dark lenses. The sun was already shining brightly and the heat of it beat down on her ivory skin. She hoped that the sun block she'd applied before leaving the hotel would be strong enough to keep her from burning. The heat here didn't allow for wearing long sleeves or pants. She'd have to see about buying the native wear until she'd built up a decent tan.

Her hazel eyes spotted a white tent west of the water's edge, behind it were the charred and splintered remains of a new structure. Anna set off in the direction of the tent. As she approached a slightly older man with dark hair and steel grey eyes emerged. He smiled and Anna sighed.

"Anna so good to see you again my dear," he said with enthusiasm.

"Hello Ian."

"Come inside have a look."

"Not so fast Ian, I wanted to sit down first, go over the contract and I want it signed, before I even look at your vase," Anna said, her voice was cold and demanded no argument.

"Very well, since you insist. I had hoped we could keep this civil; that perhaps we might patch things up between the two of us," Ian said with a sigh.

"We can be civil once I know that my credit in identifying this thing is assured. I won't let you cheat me again."

"It wasn't my intention to cheat you Anna. It was..."

"Save it Ian, I'm not interested. Your intent or not you've done nothing to correct the error. You wanted the credit for yourself and you got it. I understand that now. You have to understand that I can't live with a person who I can't trust," Anna stated.

Ian nodded. Turning he led her into the tent where his desk had been situated. "Here you go, all nice and official," he stated, sliding a stack of pages across the desk to her.

Anna picked them up and looked them over making sure she was satisfied with the wording before signing. She passed them back, watched as he signed. "Thank you. I expect a copy of it by day's end."

"You'll get it my dear I promise," he assured her. "Come, the vase is in the back as are the rest of the team. I hope you can shed some light on it; the others are stumped."

Anna followed Ian through a hanging sheet separating his work space from the dig site. Here three men stood gathered around a table studying the artifact.

"Gentlemen I believe you all know Dr. Annalynn Gallagher."

The trio turned from their work to greet her. Anna stepped passed Ian to join them at the table. She studied the vase with fascination. He was right the style was authentic to the culture of 18th 19th century BC for the area. Well-crafted and magnificent. The image it depicted was indeed Grecian in appearance. The image that of Zeus sitting on his throne on top Mount Olympus gazing down at man thunderbolt poised to strike.

"Have you dated it yet?" She asked.

"We were just about to do so. We've run tests on the material and it is consistent with the authentic." Omar said.

"Well, then let's finish the test and see what it says."

24

"It is the genuine article." Dr. Omar Bashir said with surprise.

Anna's eyes lit with excitement. "Have you found anything else in the excavation site?"

"No, it's like the vase fell out of the sky," Hakeem said with a laugh.

"Well, then I guess we'll need to expand the search area. I'll let Ian know," Anna stated. Turning she tried to ignore Dr. Manal's icy glare. The Jordanian was raised Muslim he did not approve of a woman being involved. She headed back into the front portion of the tent.

"Well its official the vase is real. It was made some time during the 18th or 19th century BC. We'll have to expand the search area."

"You're sure?" Ian questioned.

"Yes, I suggest you let your employer know. I'm going to get started documenting it, trying to sort out where it's from," Anna said before moving back into the work area. The trio of scientists had already returned to the dig site. They were busy at work searching for additional artifacts.

Alone Anna pulled out one of her sketch books and set to the task of drawing the vase. She drew first an image of the whole then went in for more fine point detail work of the art work itself. Something about the city Zeus overlooked was familiar to her, though what, she couldn't quite place. Anna shrugged she'd come back to it later. With the sketches done she took photos of the vase then numbered and dated it for the museum's records.

25

Dr. Ian Broody picked up his phone and punched in the number for Mr. York, he hoped the man was in a good mood.

"What?" the answer was cold and irritated. Ian repressed a curse, if it was possible Russell seemed more agitated than the last time they spoke.

"Russell its Ian I have some news on your vase."

"Well?"

"The vase is a genuine artifact from the 18th or 19th century BC. My team has begun looking for any further pieces in the area. I'm afraid we'll have to shut your building project down for the foreseeable future."

"Broody is there any chance we can make this artifact go away?" A second voice asked.

Ian coughed as his lungs backed up with air. He hadn't realized he'd been on speaker phone. Ian knew who the other voice was. He'd never heard it before but it could be no other than Russell's employer Mr. Halden. The thought of it made his blood run cold. The man made Russell seem like a teddy bear by comparison. "I'm afraid not sir, too many people are aware of the discovery." Ian replied, he hoped the answer didn't provoke the man's wrath.

"Understood. But hear me Broody you keep your people out of the construction site."

"Yes sir."

"Good man. Keep us posted." Russell requested.

"Of course," Ian assured him before the phone went dead. Ian set it down and drew a breath. He'd managed to avoid getting threatened again. He figured that meant things had gone well enough. Ian wished for a moment he could walk away from the project and Mr. Russell's services but knew it was impossible. He'd made his bed years ago now he had to lie in it.

26

Anna sat at the small table in her suite, at the King David Hotel, studying the image of the city from the vase. She knew the image, she was sure of it. With care she set the image on her scanner and copied it to her laptop. She enlarged the image and printed it then began a thorough search of her records for something to place it.

Her eyes began to grow heavy as fatigue set in. Anna yawned and glancing at the clock she groaned. She'd been at it now for well over three hours. Anna went back to the beginning of the paragraph having lost her place and cursed. She clicked on the image file connected to the report and smiled. Ian wasn't going to believe what she'd just found.

Picking up her phone Anna dialed his number she hoped he was still up. The phone rang three times before she heard the familiar click of the line connecting.

"Anna it's late," he said a hint of annoyance in his voice.

"I know it is Ian, but you've got to see what I found."

"Can it wait until morning?"

"I suppose it can but you won't want it to," Anna murmured.

"I'm on my way," he assured her then hung up.

Anna set her cell phone down and printed up the notes as well as the image on file. She set the pages on top of her sketch pad. Turning she checked her appearance in the mirror and sighed. She'd forgotten she'd changed into her bed clothes. There was no way she was meeting with him as she was. Rising from her chair Anna crossed the suite to her dresser grabbed a shirt and a pair of jeans. She stepped into the bathroom to change, she just hoped she'd be ready before he got there.

27 JERUSALEM, ISRAEL
APRIL
FRIDAY
10PM

Ian stood in the elevator waiting for it to reach his destination. He checked his reflection on the mirrored surface of the car making sure he looked good. Before it dinged indicating it was approaching his stop. Satisfied with his appearance his thought drifted to Anna. What had she found? He wondered whatever it was she was excited.

Anna hadn't been this eager to see him since Ithaca. He sighed, he'd underestimated her devotion to her career and overvalued their relationship. He'd been stunned when she called off the engagement. The fact she'd insisted on a contract before working the dig infuriated him. He'd given it because she was good at what she did; but beyond that he hoped to repair the damage. Her parents had been more than understanding; apologizing for her rash behavior and trying to steer her back. So far she hadn't budged.

Ian stepped off the elevator on the fourth floor and made his way towards the junior suite Anna had been registered in. He marked it a good sign that she'd wanted to meet there as opposed to neutral territory. Maybe she was beginning to come around. Ian smiled; he hoped so. He knocked on the door to her room and waited.

"I'm coming," she called from the other side of the door. A moment later the door opened to reveal her. He noted she wore a pair of blue jeans rather than a suit and counted it a good sign. Her hazel eyes were the color of an emerald at the moment. As she looked at him they swirled and shifted becoming more blue green.

"Anna my dear you look lovely as ever," he whispered.

"Ian come in. My notes are on the table," she said coolly. He watched as the color shifted again going gray. He cursed inwardly any pleasant feeling was gone again. He followed her back to the table and took a seat.

"So, what have you got for me?" he asked switching to business for the moment.

"Well, the city image on the vase, I recognized it earlier and drew it. After running it through my files I found out why. It's Sodom," She murmured handing over her work.

Ian flipped through the file printed, studied the photo and her drawing. "I see why you said I'd not want it to wait. Remarkable. Nice work Anna. We'll widen the search tomorrow, bring in additional workers."

"Sounds good," Anna stated.

"Anna I must confess I asked you here for an ulterior motive. I had hoped that…"

"Ian, I don't want to talk about this again. I told you before I left Ithaca, that we were over and I meant it. I won't get mixed up with you again. You betrayed my trust and stole my career," she said, her voice held both pain and anger.

"Anna I…" Ian began he reached for her hands.

She pulled away from his touch. "Get out Ian; I'll see you in the morning," Anna snapped. She stormed across the room to the door and threw it open. Ian rose from his seat and made his way toward her.

"Good night my dear, rest well," he murmured then brushed a kiss on her lips. She turned from him, his lips brushing her cheek instead.

"Good night."

Ian sighed; walked out the door. "Anna please I love you, be fair." He requested.

"Fair! Who are you to speak of fair? You didn't treat me fairly," she snapped before closing the door in his face.

Ian swore before he turned and headed back toward the elevator. Given time perhaps she would see reason.

28 DEAD SEA
JULY
FRIDAY
4PM

Anna sighed as she looked over the expanse of torn up earth. She and the team had been working over three months now sifting through dirt and sand but had found no other sign of the fallen city. Ian was growing impatient and she contemplated dropping the project. Bad enough dealing with his rotten mood but he was still pressing her romantically. It frustrated her that he was slowly getting to her. She needed to get out of there regain her perspective. Between his overtures and her parents pressing her to forgive him she was slowly going mad.

Anna blinked; a different view, that was a good idea she told herself. Moving out of the hole the team was working on she made her way to a small hill near the dig site. She climbed up with care not to fall. It was a bit steep. Once on top she gazed down at the work zone. Her focus settled on the original find. Okay so there was nothing around it. If that was the case then where was the city? How had the vase gotten there? She went back over the discovery report, recalled the mention of a slight quake and tried to picture the scene in her head.

Closing her eyes she took a step back. The ground under her was soft, gave way. Anna opened her eyes as she fought for balance. She fell forward onto her hands and knees. Cursed then blew out a breath moving her hair out of her eyes. "Nice one Anna you nearly fell off the damn hill," she muttered to herself.

"Anna, are you all right dear?" Ian called from below.

"Fine," she assured him, then drew a breath, there at her finger tips sticking out of the ground was a pottery shard. "Ian I think I've got something," she shouted with excitement. She listened to the sound of rushed foot falls as Ian made his way up to her. Anna dug at the shards with her fingers unearthing the find.

"What is it?" Ian questioned as he came into view.

Anna rose to her feet and handed him the shards. "You tell me," she said her voice cool again.

"It's the same," he breathed. His voice held wonder.

Yes," Anna said with satisfaction. She watched as Ian called a halt to the work below and shouted instructions to the crew.

"Nice work Anna."

"Thanks, though it wasn't skill here that found it, just luck," Anna muttered.

"I need you to head back to the hotel and rest. I'll meet up with you in an hour or so with word on how our employer wants to proceed," Ian stated.

Anna nodded knowing there wasn't much more daylight left. Anything of note would be found tomorrow with the light of dawn.

29

Ian Broody moved away from the commotion of the workers on the hill retreating back into the tent housing his office. He pulled out his phone and punched in the number for Russell.

"Hello Ian."

"Hello Mr. York, I have good news on all fronts."

"I'm listening."

"Dr. Gallagher found the city today on a hill overlooking the site. You're work area is not of historic significance. We have moved the crew to the believed location and you should be able to restart your construction project."

"Are you sure?"

"Daylight will tell the tale but yes I am fairly certain."

"That's excellent news. Take your Dr. Gallagher out to dinner on us. Good work Ian."

"Thank you sir."

"No Ian, thank you," Russell said with a laugh before he hung up. Ian sighed with relief then smiled, today's discovery had cleaned the slate with Mr. York. He was no longer on dangerous ground, it was a huge weight off his shoulders. For the past three months his lack of progress had seen Russell's attitude get worse. Threats had become more frequent. Ian was pleased to be out of the dog house. Now if he could just get Anna to forgive him then things could get back to normal.

30

Anna crossed the thresh-hold into her junior suite. She bypassed the living area, headed straight for the bath. Her skin itched with the grit of dirt, sand, and the salt of her sweat. Flipping on the light Anna sat down on the tub ledge and untied her work boots before pulling them off and setting them in the corner with her socks tucked inside. S got to her feet and shed her work clothes before she stepped into the old claw foot tub. She turned on the faucet and sank down into the hot water.

Anna sighed as the stiffness in her joints and muscles eased. She felt the dull ache of a blooming migraine fade away as the heavy strain and tension of late receded. No more worrying over getting nowhere. Results had been produced. The dig was real. Ian was happy. Anna groaned she shouldn't care about what he felt. He hadn't considered her feelings in Ithaca. Why was she letting him get to her? They were over. Even as she told herself this, she contemplated what to wear for their meet later.

"Gah, stop it girl. He is not worth your time," Anna reminded herself. She resolved to wear a no nonsense suit and make it clear their meet was strictly business. The matter settled; Anna turned her focus to getting ready.

31

Ian made his way down the hall towards Anna's suite. He held in one hand a bouquet of long stemmed red roses. He hoped they'd be received well as he wondered what she'd be wearing. Ian knocked gently and waited for her to answer.

Russell had given him the means to take her out for a nice dinner and he planned to. They'd celebrate the find and discuss business as planned. Her mood would be more forgiving. Perhaps they could share a bottle of wine and with a little luck get back to the way things were before Ithaca.

The door opened and Ian was disappointed to see she wore a pair of neatly pressed black slacks with a white blouse and matching blazer. All business; there was nothing remotely personal or friendly to her attire. She'd drawn a line in the sand by wrapping herself in her professional armor. She meant to keep the evening work oriented. He wasn't surprised, his previous overtures since her arrival to mend their relationship had been refused with the typical cool prim and proper act Annalynn Darcy Gallagher had perfected with an art.

Ian smiled, tonight he wasn't taking no for an answer. "Good evening Anna darling you look lovely as usual," he murmured in greeting as he lifted the roses from his side to give to her. He watched with delight as a blush colored her cheeks. It was a good sign the ice she'd been closing herself in was beginning to melt.

"Ian..." she began in protest.

"A birthday present, Dr. Gallagher," he explained, cutting off her objection and giving her the space she'd been demanding since her arrival, throwing her off guard. She blinked, her hazel eyes held confusion. Ian crowed inwardly, aware she'd forgotten the day.

"Thank you," she relented. "Please, come in. I'll just go put them in some water," Anna said before she turned to see to the task leaving the door open for him.

Ian smiled as he stepped inside. He'd managed to make it past the front gate, it was a good sign. Ian took a seat on the sofa to wait for her. His eyes skimmed over the room taking in the sight of her domain. Reacquainting himself with her space. He noted it was immaculately clean, he wondered if she'd been bothering the staff here with her insistent requests for fresh towels as she had in Ithaca. He spotted her work space and noted that it was the only area in the suite that was not in perfect order. Anna was a creature of habit and it made it easier for him to get past her defenses, because he knew and understood them. It didn't hurt either that her parents were in his corner. Mommy and Daddy's opinion pulled a lot of weight where Anna was concerned.

Ian rose from his seat when Anna reentered the room. He studied her and noted she'd drawn her resolve back, her hazel eyes now gray. He sighed with disappointment but let the matter go. He'd known that winning Anna over was not going to be an easy task.

"All right, I'm all set. Let's go, Dr. Broody," she said in a rush. Ian nodded following after her hiding his disappointment at her using his last name. She was creating distance again, closing the breach he'd managed to create. It seemed his date for the evening would be Miss prim and proper not his loving fiancé. He gave himself a point though, Anna was not one to rush, that she was now, spoke of an inner conflict. Good he'd take any sign of weakness in her image as proof that he was getting to her.

The pair moved down the hall and stepped into the elevator headed for the lobby.

"So, where are we headed?" she asked with interest.

"The Focaccia Bar."

"Ian…"

"Russell's treat for your work today. I thought we could have a bite while we spoke, maybe toast the find Dr. Gallagher," Ian stated all business knowing that to get where he wanted he had to show no hints of his actual intent. Anna was like a wild bird, he'd have to draw her out with care before he could catch her.

"Okay, if Mr. York is paying I'm not going to pass it up, Dr. Broody," Anna said with a smile. Ian watched as her gray eyes swirled and shifted becoming an icy blue. He offered her his arm and she took it without hesitation following his lead settling into old habits.

The pair made the short walk from the hotel to the restaurant. Upon stepping inside the hostess escorted them to a small private booth separated from the rest of the patrons. Anna let his arm go, sliding into one side as Ian sat down opposite her. He watched as she withdrew into herself forgetting him for a moment.

"Do you like the table?" Ian asked drawing her back. Now that they were here he'd not allow her to retreat from him. Anna didn't know it yet but they were going to make their peace tonight and get back to where they'd been before Ithaca.

"It's nice, though I'm not sure we need something so private," Anna said with a hint of trepidation in her voice.

"We can't have anyone overhearing about the dig," Ian stated as the waiter approached.

She nodded. "Fair enough," Anna relented and turned her attention to the menu. While she was distracted Ian ordered her favorite desert and a bottle of champagne. He then turned his attention to the menu.

"Russell was pleased to learn the site for his building was not of any historical significance. He's looking forward to seeing what we unearth tomorrow. Thank you for your help Anna, I'd not have found it without you," Ian murmured.

"I didn't do anything Dr. Broody. It was all luck," she corrected as the waiter returned with the champagne and strawberries.

"Then let's toast to luck," Ian said and he handed her a glass as he raised his own. She raised hers and they drank the glass. Ian refilled the flutes careful not to spill and watched as Anna ate one of the berries. "So Dr. Gallagher how is your family?" he asked as he set the glasses on the table.

"Mother and Father are doing well, they asked me to say hello by the way. They miss you. I haven't heard from Terra. It's weird I normally get some sort of token from her today."

"I'm sure she hasn't forgotten. It probably just got delayed in the mail. Tell your parents I said hello please. I miss them too," Ian stated with a polite smile.

"I will," she assured him as the waiter returned with a plate holding a slice of French silk pie. "Oh, wow, that looks amazing. Ian you shouldn't have done this. I haven't had desert first since before Ithaca. I've been trying to eat better." Anna commented. Ian grinned pleased to see she'd appreciated the choice.

"It's your day Anna, in more ways than one. It's all right to indulge," he murmured before lifting his champagne glass again. "To you, Anna, on your birthday."

Ian watched with delight as she lifted her glass to the toast and drank down the sparking liquid. He collected her glass yet again and refilled it and his own. Watching as she ate another strawberry before picking up a fork. She lifted the first fork full to her lips and tasted, savoring the flavor of it. Anna made a pleasured throaty sound that went right to Ian's groin as he recalled other places she made such sounds.

He looked on as she blushed prettily and looked up to the waiter rattling off her order. Ian made his own request and handed the menus to the man, his gaze focused on Anna and her desert. He fell silent as she ate, allowing her to enjoy the treat in peace. His own appetite for her growing stronger as he watched her. When she was done he spoke again.

"I instructed the team to be at the site tomorrow before dawn. I'm hoping to unearth as much of the site as possible before sunset tomorrow. Maybe we'll get lucky and find something truly enlightening. I don't expect you to be there quite so early. I'm hoping that they'll have found something specific for you to focus your considerable talents on." Ian said turning the conversation back to the reason for which they had come. The easiest way to get past Anna's defenses he had learned was to keep her on her toes and unsure where you were leading her.

"Sounds good, I'm wondering how large the ruins will be and hoping that we'll find something to explain the Grecian god on the pottery. None of my research on Sodom indicates any connection to the origin of Zeus."

"I know and if we can prove that it is. Well, I'm sure I don't need to tell you the magnitude of the discovery."

"It would be like finding the Ark of the Covenant or the Grail," Anna said with wonder.

"Indeed. To the dig," Ian exclaimed as he lifted his crystal flute. He watched as Anna picked up hers.

"To great discoveries," She answered before drinking the alcohol. She set the empty cup down and picked up another strawberry as the waiter returned with their meal. He set their plates down in front of them then took the berries and champagne away along with the glasses. He replaced them with goblets setting a bottle of red wine between them. He asked if they'd need anything else and Ian shook his head. He watched with delight as Anna dug into her meal and drank the wine.

Ian started in on his own food taking his time slowing her progress with various questions and comments, she responded to each with a pleasant tone her Dr. Broody's had slowly become Ian and a smile he'd not seen in months returned to grace her lips. He smiled with pleasure and struggled not to gloat; he had her now.

When she was done Ian asked for the check and then with care escorted Anna back to her room.

"How are you feeling my dear?" he whispered as she opened the door.

"I feel good. A little tipsy I think," she murmured.

"Would you like me to make you some coffee?" he asked gently.

"That would be nice."

Ian stepped into the room and headed for the kitchen starting a pot of coffee for her. As he waited for it to heat a knock sounded and he crossed to the door. Opening it he accepted a small box which he walked into the living room area where she sat on the couch. Opening it he revealed a small Terminus cake. "To go with the coffee," he explained before returning to the kitchen. He returned a moment later with two mugs. He handed her one and sipped his own before slicing off a piece of the desert for her.

They shared the desert and when the coffee was gone she spoke again.

"Thank you for a lovely evening Ian it was nice, I'm feeling a bit sleepy and I think you should go now. I'll see you in the morning though," she murmured before rising from her seat. She made her way to the door and opened it for him. Ian rose from his seat and followed her to the door.

"Happy birthday Anna," he whispered. He reached out with his right hand to caress her cheek and his lips met with hers. Kissing her as he'd wanted to for months. She tasted of coffee and desert and he found that the small taste was not enough. She gasped startled by him but melted into him accepting him as she always had.

His hands sank deep in her hair pulling her head back as his teeth nipped at her lower lip asking for more. She gave it without hesitation and he dove deeper devouring her lips as he closed the door. He backed her up into the wall pressing his advantage, hands seeking warm skin. He overwhelmed her senses conquering her anew and thrilling in her surrender. As he tore away the professional attire Ian laughed; Anna was his again.

32

Anna woke with a pounding headache, her stomach queasy. She blinked. Her lashes felt heavy and gritty. Her eyes refused to focus. She felt like she had cotton in her mouth and realized to her horror that she was hung over. She closed her eyes and searched her mind trying to recall the night before. It was as she lay there, she became aware of a strange weight across her belly and another at her hip. Opening her eyes she noted she was laying on the wrong side of the bed and looking to her right she gasped with disbelief.

Ian, God, no this couldn't be happening. How drunk had she been last night. What had she done? Anna slipped free of his grasp with care not to wake him and wrapped one of the blankets about her. She crept from the bedroom to the bathroom and switched on the shower; needing to wash in the worst way. She let the hot water beat against her as she scrubbed her skin and tried not to cry.

How had he gotten to her? She'd been so careful to avoid his advances since her arrival. Yet here she was with the mother of all hangovers waking up naked in his arms and sneaking around in her own suite praying he didn't wake. It was mortifying.

Once she was clean Anna slipped out of the shower and wrapped herself in a towel, she turned her attention to drying her hair as she let the tears fall. She hated herself for letting him get that close to her again. Hated him for being able to get past her defenses. Some birthday she grumbled to herself as the bathroom door opened behind her letting in cool air from the room beyond. She spun to face the intruder, her hazel eyes the color of steel.

"Get out Ian," She demanded not about to let him near her again. She watched with disgust as he crossed the floor to her side. He reached out to touch her and she pulled away from him.

"Anna darling, please must you be so cool this morning last night you were far more pleasant. Wild and willing, eager for my touch," he whispered as his fingers ran down her arm.

"Last night wasn't me. It was a mistake and changes nothing." Anna snapped retreating from him again. She realized to late her mistake as it left her back against the wall trapped.

"You're wrong my dear it changes everything. It proves that you still love me," he murmured. She felt his hands settle on her bare shoulders before he brushed a familiar kiss on her forehead. Anna denied him further access. She shrugged loose of his grasp.

"No, it doesn't. Go!" She turned her head looking away from his gaze.

"Look at me Anna, you know I love you," he breathed, his lips brushed against her temple then trailed down her face. Lips parted and his teeth nipped her left ear lobe in the way he knew gave her pleasure before moving down her throat. Anna trembled as his right hand brushed against her face turning her so that their eyes met. His fingers brushed through her damp hair sinking into the blond tresses to caress her neglected ear. She felt his other hand clench wet towel seeking skin.

Anna pushed against his chest seeking space. Her mind clouding under the assault as her body responded to his. "I can't think," she whispered with fear.

"Then don't" Ian demanded, before his lips met with hers taking greedily what he desired of her. Anna's heart hammered in her chest as she yielded to his kiss; giving him what he silently ordered of her. She shook with a confused mass of feeling, a strange mix of fear and desire as her mind was flooded with images of the night before.

Anna's hands which had gone still pressed against him; breaking her free from his grasp as she slid off the wall. "I can't do this again," she whispered before retreating past him back into the bedroom. She was grateful that he didn't pursue her further instead she heard the shower come on as she crossed to the closet and dressed for the dig site. Ready to face the day she moved into the living room and cursed at the site of breakfast, laid out on a cart; no doubt brought up by room service.

Cocky bastard had probably placed the order last night; knowing he'd be here in the morning. It irked her to no end he'd managed to get to her. That he'd been able to stir her up despite her protests. It wasn't fair. Her thoughts drifted to what he'd said. "You still love me…You know I love you."

No. She didn't love him. Couldn't. Not after what he'd done in Ithaca. How could he claim to love her when he could so completely betray her trust that way? "Men need to prove they are the better workers Anna, my dear you shouldn't be so hard on Ian, he loves you and will take care of you," her mother's voice murmured in the back of her mind.

Anna sighed. Maybe they were all right and she was overreacting. Perhaps she should forgive him and move on with their life together. Put the ring back on her finger and walk down the aisle in the spring as they'd planned. The thought cut her heart deeply. How could she?

Anna walked over to the cart and noted a package sitting next to one of the plates. An envelope was tied to the front of it. A familiar handwriting on it made her smile. She pulled the envelope free from the package and tore open the back pulling the card free. She read the card quietly to herself and flipped it open to see what her sister had written.

"To my dear sister on her special day. Well, Anna it's been another year I hope it was a good one. I wanted to let you know I'm proud of you for standing up to Mother and Father on the Ian thing. I know it must be difficult for you. Don't give up on yourself or a chance at finding a man who will love you for who you are rather than whom you pretend to be. Good luck in all your endeavors and I look forward to seeing you upon your return. Love always Terra." Anna brushed tears from her eyes before tucking the card and the package in her bag for the day; she'd look at it later.

She turned and looked up as Ian walked into the room. "Hungry?" he asked.

"Not really," she replied.

"I got your favorite," he whispered as he reached out to brush his fingers through her hair. Anna stepped away from him and lifted a hand to prevent him from coming any closer.

"Dr. Broody please let's keep this professional," she murmured setting the envelope down.

"Who was the card from?"

"Terra, you were right it got delayed. I should get going. See you at the dig," Anna said her voice cool as ice and calm. Without waiting for a reply she tuned and left.

33

Ian listened to the sound of the door shutting behind her and picked up the envelope on the tray. He studied the delicate script for a moment before balling the paper up and tossing it with disgust in the fireplace. He wondered silently as he ate his meal what Anna's meddling sister had written to her. He cursed Terra and her interfering in his business yet again. The other woman was Anna's opposite, wild and willful, unwilling to com-promise and fast to speak her mind. In short she was a rebel and the black sheep of her family. Ian had hated her from the moment they met and she'd made no secret of her own distaste of him.

Ian sighed as he finished his meal. He'd been so close. Anna had been on the edge. If he'd just been able to assault her senses once more that morning he'd have had her. Instead he'd given her the space she demanded not wanting to press her too far and had come to find her walls back in place again.

He blamed Terra for the change. Only her sister could get to her that fast. He wondered what the older Gallagher sister had sent Anna but dismissed the matter. He'd find out later, he was sure of it. For now he needed to focus on the dig there was lots to be done.

He'd have plenty of opportunities to get Anna back in his bed as the work progressed. Anna didn't know it yet but one of the prizes he'd walk away with at the end of this excavation was her.

34

SODOM RUINS NEAR DEAD SEA
JULY
SATURDAY
10AM

Anna stepped out of her rental car and made her way toward the hill were the excavation team was hard at work. She smiled as she tucked her sister's gift back in her bag. Leave it to Darcy to send her something off the wall and mildly embarrassing. She chuckled, as she thought of her reaction when she looked at the paperbacks scandalous cover. She'd read the back cover for Heart of Glass and flipped open the cover to the teaser page. The whole thing had drawn her in with ease. She knew she'd be reading it that night before bed.

Anna had never heard of C.J. Nichols before; as romance was not her normal read but the situation the lead character was in hit a little too close to home and Anna wondered yet again if the rumors about her sister's gift for foresight were true. Terra had a spooky way of knowing what she needed and when without them seeing each other or even speaking for months. Anna contemplated calling her but decided that it could wait a bit, she wasn't ready to discuss last night's debacle just yet.

She trembled knowing if her parents got wind of it she'd never hear the end of their arguments that she go back to Ian. It frustrated her to no end that the man had them in his corner. It wasn't right. She felt wretched and did her best to avoid the priest and rabbi added to the team, she didn't feel like getting into another religious battle this morning. What she wanted at the moment was to go back to her room and forget that the day had begun.

Anna straightened her shoulders and lifted her chin. Like hell she would do that. She refused to let Ian see, that he'd gotten to her; that her resolve had been shaken by his efforts if even for a moment. She was a professional and she'd do her job as usual nothing had changed just like she said. He'd taken advantage of her plain and simple. She'd be more careful around him from now on. Problem easily solved, she assured herself as she walked toward the crew.

"Omar good morning how is it going?" she asked politely.

"It goes well. We've unearthed the main gates and the front portion of the outer wall. It's impressive Dr. Gallagher."

"Wonderful. Where do you want me?" She questioned.

"Inside the wall, we're starting to find structures. Your skills would be much welcome there. I've got Dr. Manal working on the wall for now, so he should stay out of your way."

"Good, all right then, let's get started," Anna said and she followed the Israeli through the gateway into the lost city to begin the task of identifying and cataloging the artifacts of the find.

35

SODOM RUINS NEAR DEAD SEA
AUGUST
MONDAY
2PM

Ian knelt on the cold stone floor of a large room that the team had labeled the city temple. His field brush ran over the edge of a thick stone slab with strange letters carved in it. He'd been working on it now for over a week and had yet to identify the writing. The altar, as he'd named it, fascinated him. It was eight feet long and over six feet wide. Raised on steps so that the other main point of interest in the chamber looked on it at eyelevel. They stood well over ten feet high sculpted with a care and precision that the people of the 18th to 19th century B.C. did not possess and yet the carbon test dated it as true to their time. Ten of them together forming a perfect half circle looking on like sentinels at whatever took place in here.

What was it used for? Why was it so large? What was the significance of the Greek gods and goddesses looking on it so intently? What was it they observed? What did the writing say? All these questions circled round in his mind and yet they did nothing to quiet his rioting emotions.

He lifted his gaze from the writing to study the source of his anger. Anna worked near the foot of the statues a pencil in one hand sketch book across her knees capturing the images. She'd been refusing his attempts to reconnect since her birthday. Keeping her distance and treating him as nothing more than a colleague; it was driving him mad. He wanted her back in his bed where she belonged. His ring on her finger and preparing once again for their wedding in April.

Ian bit back a curse. As close as they'd been working together he'd have figured by now this nonsense about Ithaca would have been put behind them. Her parents had tried to reason with her but she'd stopped answering their calls. Whatever it was her sister had sent her he didn't have a clue but he blamed Terra for his inability to win over Anna. Ian felt his hands itch with an all too familiar need to touch her and he growled in frustration at his inability to do so.

He watched as she rose from the floor and closed her sketch book. Her gaze met his stare and her eyes he noted were yet again the color of steel. Damn woman was never in any mood but angry.

"What do you think it means that the statues are here looking at the altar?" Ian asked, trying yet again to engage her. She crossed to the stone slab and circled it running her fingers over it.

"I don't know. We've found very little in the way of blood stains on it. I don't think it was for human sacrifice as some have suggested Dr. Broody but I can't be sure. I just know it's odd," she replied. Her voice as usual was all business no nonsense Miss prim and proper and it enraged him.

Ian pictured himself reaching across the slab and drawing her down on it to him. Pressing her down and closing the distance between them, kissing her, breaking through that damn wall she'd built around her and taking what he hungered for where she was concerned. But before he could even think to move she spoke.

"I'm done here, I'll be moving on to one of the other locations. I'm sure you can handle this," she stated before she walked out not waiting for a response.

36

Anna sat at her desk looking through the photos she'd taken earlier in the day at the dig site. They'd unearthed the king's palace earlier that week and within it she'd discovered a second temple. This one had been different from the one for the main city. She'd found graven images there as well of the Greek gods and goddesses but instead of the ten statues they'd found in the city temple, she'd found a carved relief depicting many others. In the same chamber she'd found on one of the walls a map of the kingdom. It depicted the locations of Gomorrah and the other plains cities ruled over by the king.

Then there had been the riddle. She stared at it now, trying to make sense of the writing. "There has to be more to it," she muttered to herself for the 5th time in two hours. She'd been over the line of text more times than she could count since finding it and was still no closer to understanding it. Anna turned her head, cracking her neck and easing the tension that had built in her shoulders. It was time for a break she decided.

Rising from her seat she was startled at the sound of a knock at her door. Anna sighed. Glancing at the time she crossed the floor to the door and peered through the peek hole. She groaned inwardly at the sight of the man on the other side of the door. She'd been avoiding him for weeks now but realized tonight there would be no putting him off. He was there about the dig.

Opening the door she stood in the threshold refusing to allow him entrance, he'd not invade her personal space again. "Good evening Dr. Broody," she said politely.

"Dr. Gallagher, have you had any luck with the riddle?" Ian questioned.

"No, I'm convinced it's not all there, it doesn't make sense as it is." Anna replied stating her belief.

"Any theories?" Ian questioned.

"I suspect that the rest is in Gomorrah."

"Why there?"

"They are sister cities and I'm willing to bet that the king had a similar palace there, that maybe the other gods and goddesses will be depicted there as well."

"What if you're wrong?"

"Then I'm missing something in front of me."

"Can I come in and take a look perhaps I can help to solve the mystery," Ian offered.

"No, Ian you won't be coming in here again. You've abused my trust both here and in Ithaca. I will not let you back into my life again. We are colleagues now; nothing more. You've ensured that with what you did on my birthday."

"Anna, I..."

"You don't love me Ian, not really, so let me go," Anna requested.

"How can you say that, we were to be married?"

"If you loved me you'd have understood that stealing my credit for Ithaca would have hurt me. You'd have known that waking hung over to find you in my bed would have been looked upon as an abuse of our relationship. You don't know me and therefore don't love me PhD. Broody. Now if you want me to stay here and finish the work I've begun I suggest you leave and let this matter go. Good night," Anna stated her voice cool as winter's snow.

"You wouldn't leave."

"Yes, I will."

"You're not being rational, Anna dear. I'll speak with you when you're in a better mood. Good night," Ian said then he turned and walked down the hall.

Anna watched him go before closing the door. She blew out a breath and slid down the door, tears pricked her eyes, she hoped that she'd done the right thing. Turning her head she eased the tension there and assured herself she had. Closing the file with her photos from the dig, Anna settled into her bed with a well-worn copy of Heart of Glass. She'd read it more times than she could count and the subsequent sequels in the trilogy by C.J. Nichols.

Opening the cover she told herself that the answers to the riddle lay in the ruins of Gomorrah. In time she'd discover them as well.

PART 4

DREAMS END

37

The familiar trill of his cell phone drew Lance Roman from his light sleep. He lifted his head from the comfort of his soft pillow and reached over his sleeping fiancé to the offending object. He clicked the button to silence the phone as he drew it to him.

"Detective Roman," he said in a hushed tone, in a bid to avoid waking the sleeping beauty at his side.

"Sorry for the hour detective but we've got another one," a young man's voice stated uneasily.

Lance ran a hand through his red hair as he closed tired blue eyes. He was really getting sick of these early morning calls disturbing what peaceful sleep he managed to find at night. "You're sure?" he questioned as Dana stirred beside him lifting her head, brown eyes wide with question.

"Afraid so," the young man replied.

"Where are you?" Lance questioned as he opened his eyes again and threw back his covers.

"Rock Creek Cemetery."

"I'll be there in twenty," Lance stated before hanging up the call.

"Him again," Dana asked as she sat up behind him.

"Yeah, another cemetery," Lance said with resignation.

"That makes three," Dana said with a yawn.

"I know; we better get a move on." Lance stated. The pair moved away from the bed and busied themselves with getting changed. Once dressed and armed, the pair stepped out of Lance's home and climbed into their shared squad car. Lance backed the car off the drive onto the street and set off for Rock Creek Cemetery.

38

WASHINGTON DC
JULY
SUNDAY
7AM

The early morning air was cool and damp but the rising sun had already begun to burn off the evening dew. It wouldn't be long before the summer heat beat down on the world below. As Lance made his way towards the yellow crime scene tape in the distance, the distinct scent of freshly trampled grass filled the air, as he walked past a statue of the grim reaper. Lance repressed a shiver. He hated cemeteries. There was always some lingering sense of darkness hanging in this place for the dead. Behind him Dana hummed softly to herself. It gave him a strange sense of ease to know that she was not comfortable with their current surroundings either.

As the pair drew near the crowd ahead Lance spotted the elaborate graven image of an angel looking over the burial grounds in the direction of the victim.

"Seems like our guy's got a thing for having angels watching him as he works," Dana commented from behind him.

Lance turned and studied his partner for a moment before moving on. Her brown eyes were heavy with sleepiness and he worried she'd not be able to shake off the tired of being dragged from their bed yet again in the middle of the night. "Yeah, this makes two out of three. The first one was near a church. It was gargoyles looking on there instead, right?"

"Right but they are angels also, just fallen ones," Dana stated before taking a sip from the coffee they'd stopped for on the way.

The pair fell silent as they ducked under the crime scene tape and crossed the grassy field headed to where the victim's body lay spread out. Lance studied the young woman with a growing sense of disquiet. A pair of lifeless hazel eyes stared up at him wide with horror. Pale skin was stained with crimson where the killer had left cuts beneath her eyes leaving the illusion of bloody tears. A crown was set upon her brow of golden serpents. A long flowing crimson gown covered her battered flesh just like the previous two victims had worn.

"It's confirmed that makes three," Dana stated, her voice grim.

"Right, we've definitely got a serial killer on our hands," Lance said with disgust. He turned his focus from the victim to the officer standing watch over the scene. "What do we know so far?" Lance questioned.

"Well, the grounds keeper found her a little after 5am. He called it in and I and my partner arrived here on scene first. I contained the scene as best I could, my partner's over with the grounds keeper trying to calm him down. Poor old guy isn't handling what he saw well. When I saw her I called the chief and told him you should be here; seeing as your lead detective on this thing."

"Where's the forensic team?"

"CSI is in route."

"Okay, nice work…"

"Detective Roman?" A familiar voice called from behind. It was warm and inviting, and managed to convey both concern and excitement at the same time. Lance cursed; he'd hoped she'd not show until after the coroner had carted off the body. It wasn't his night, it seemed, Lance told himself. Lance turned and did his best to steer the over eager reporter away from the crime scene.

"Miss Walsh." He said politely as he extended his hand to the bleach blonde haired woman with sharp brown eyes.

"Pamela." She corrected, her crimson lips curved into a seductive smile as she tried to look past him in the direction of the yellow tape.

"All right Pamela, what brings you out to a cemetery at this hour?" Lance questioned leading her further from the actual scene as the CSI team headed toward the body.

"I heard a call over the police band for a homicide. Does your being here mean that we've got a serial killer on the loose?"

"Miss Walsh, I will not comment on what we have here as of now, because it's not clear yet," Lance stated.

"Pamela," she said hurt, those full lips forming a sulky pout. "Is this one like the others?" She asked.

"No comment. Look, you'll get a statement as soon as there is one to give. For now Pamela, do us a favor, let our people do their jobs and give the dead a moment of peace."

"I want whatever you have first detective, you owe me," Pamela reminded, whiskey brown eyes demanding his agreement.

"You'll get it," Lance assured her, before turning back to the crime scene. He glanced back and watched with satisfaction as the overzealous reporter departed.

"Pamela?" Dana questioned watching as the slinky blonde made her way back toward the local news van.

"Yeah, you know Miss Walsh, always looking for the big story. I got her out of our hair for now."

"Good."

"Come on, we'll need to go speak with the grounds keeper. We should take care of it while the team works the scene."

Dana nodded and together the pair made their way to where the officer's partner sat with an older man speaking in hushed voices.

39 WASHINGTON DC
JULY
SUNDAY
9AM

Dana sat at her desk reading over her notes from the grounds keeper interview. She yawned as she listened to the rhythmic sound of Lance typing up his notes and their report.

"You about done?" she questioned.

"Yeah," he answered distractedly.

"Good maybe we can still catch a little sleep."

"Not likely shift starts in an hour."

"I'm not working today Lance, remember," Dana stated with a hint of annoyance.

She watched as he lifted his head and his blue eyes met with her brown ones. There was puzzlement in them for a moment before his memory clicked into place. "That's right you're out until Wednesday with Gena. Sorry, not all here," he said with a shrug.

"No problem, I'll be busy with dress fittings and flowers, are you still good with the colors we discussed?" Dana asked.

"Of course, I just want you to be happy, Dana. Go have fun with Gena." He answered with a smile and a wink.

Danna got to her feet and shouldered her purse. "Thank you, see you later."

Lance got to his feet and grabbed her by the arm slowing her departure. He drew her into his embrace.

"Bye sweetie, I'll miss you," he murmured before he brushed a kiss on her lips. She melted into it taking the kiss deeper and then drew back, turned and walked away.

"To keep you warm until I get back," She explained over her shoulder then she walked out into the morning light.

40

HE watched with anticipation as Detective Murphy stepped out of the police station alone and crossed the lot in the direction where her unmarked cruiser was parked. Her strides were long and full of purpose. He wondered where she was going as he thrilled in the fact he was so close to the lovely Dana. After seeing her at the church he'd given some serious thought into taking her and fashioning her into one of his Furies surely she would endure the transformation and be worthy to stand by his side.

The voice that seemed to come from his knife he wielded had not approved of the choice so he'd taken another instead and left her on display for the detective and her partner. HE listened to the clicking of her heels on the pavement as she passed him and pictured covering her mouth with the chloroform rag in his pocket and dragging her into his car. Driving off with her in tow and taking her back to his lair. He felt his groin tighten at the thought of it. He'd not shape this one into a Fury as the others before since it was clear his knife had no desire to taste her. No this one he would keep. He felt a growing hunger to possess her.

She froze mid-step; turned and looked around as if uneasy HE trembled. Was she aware of him? Did she feel him now watching her dreaming of her? See me, his mind urged even as the knife concealed in his jacket warned him against pursuing her further. It whispered for patience and promised that in time he would have her but now he must continue to fashion their Furies. HE let his gaze move from the woman to the lot itself and she moved on. Slipping into her car and pulling out

So far neither she nor her partner had picked up on him following them. They both seemed too wrapped up in each other to notice the well-mannered stranger in their midst. Perhaps that was why his knife held no interest in her. She was not untouched as the others had been before he got his hands on them. Whatever the reason he was glad of the blades lack of interest. It meant she wouldn't have to die.

HE pulled out onto the road and followed Detective Murphy at a safe distance back to her shared apartment with detective Roman. She stepped inside. As he watched and waited HE wondered if she was aware that a few of her things were missing. Could she feel his presence in this place, her apartment. HE pressed a hand against the pocket which held a slip of paper with the scent of her perfume. Considered drawing it out to smell but before HE could, she emerged from the house. Gone was the dress suit of work, in its place was a simple blue cotton sundress and a pair of sandals. She slipped into the car, backed off the driveway and set off once more.

HE wound his way through traffic, careful to never get to close to Dana's car. When she came to a stop again it was outside a nice looking loft apartment building. She shouldered her purse and an overnight bag and made her way up the walk. Before she even reached the door it opened. A young woman stepped outside into the day- light. Her fiery red hair was pulled back into a long neat tail. Ivory limbs wrapped around Dana in a welcome embrace.

So this was Gena. HE eyed her with interest HE'D heard the name in passing but until now had not seen her. She was a looker this one so much like his lady. She wore a vivid green silk tank top with black shorts and matching sandals. A pair of dark shades hid her eyes from his view. She greeted her friend with excitement before taking her overnight bag and tossing it inside. She locked the door then eyed the cruiser.

HE cracked his window enough to hear their conversation.

"Were not taking that thing are we?" Gena questioned.

"Not unless you want to," Dana answered.

"I'll pass. Come on I'll drive," Gena stated.

As she rounded her sleek Porsche, Gena lowered her shades to reveal a pair of amazing hazel eyes. HE felt his fingers begin to itch as his body became painfully aroused. Within his jacket the knife practically sang with a delight all its own.

"Don't see me yet," HE whispered. He watched with joy as she shrugged, turned and got into the car. A moment later HE was back on the road following them.

41

Dana groaned inwardly as she tried on yet another wedding gown only to find it wasn't the one. She and Gena had been at it for over two hours and while she'd seen a few that had potential and most of them had looked good on her she had yet to find one that cried take me home I'm the one.

"Okay, I've got one more with the empire waist line that you like. It's a little more than you were looking to spend but I thought we'd give it a shot. " the sales associate said as she hung up yet another gown for her.

"Thanks," Dana said trying to stay positive, if it didn't work, there were other dress shops she could go to, it just meant a little more work than she'd planned on. Gena took the dress from the sales woman and closed the door. She took it off the hanger with care and after finding the opening from the bottom lifted it up over Dana's head and watched as the delicate white chiffon slid down her frame into place over the corset style strapless bra and bridal slip.

Dana waited impatiently as her best friend and maid of honor fastened the back of the gown. She wondered for a moment, how it looked, before Gena spoke.

"Okay your set," she said as she blew out a breath.

"Thanks Gena you're the best," Dana whispered as trying as this had been for her it was exhausting for Gena as she'd been dressing and undressing her since they got there. On feet that aced from standing on the stores poorly cushioned heels for two hours during the fitting, Dana stepped out of the dressing room out on to the fitting stage.

"Oh now that is lovely, here let's try this veil and then you can look," the sales woman said with a smile. She handed a two tier elbow length white veil to Gena who stuck it in Dana's hair.

Dana turned and when she saw herself in the mirror her mouth fell open. There it was that wow she'd been looking for. The soft flowing gown of white was gathered below the bust and pleats hung below the empire waist to create an elegant sheath that hugged her curves in all the right places. Sparkling rhinestones and sequins adorned the neckline giving the gown the extra sparkle the other had been missing.

"You look like a goddess," Gena said with amazement.

"I feel like one," Dana purred. "This is it. I'll knock Lance on his ass with it," Dana said with a laugh. "How much out of my price range is it?" Dana questioned. She flipped over the tag and drew a breath nearly a hundred.

"Don't even think about it Dana, you're getting that dress. I'll cover the difference," Gena stated before her friend had a chance to talk herself out of it. Dana wept.

"Did I ever tell you you're the greatest?" She asked her friend.

"Once or twice," Gena answered as she hugged the bride to be.

"Well, I'm saying it again you're the best Gena, come on let's see what we can find to go with this for you."

"I think I've got just the dress for this," the sales associate said. She turned and left the pair to themselves for a moment. They were both admiring the gown when she returned with a long blue chiffon dress. She handed it to Gena and bid her try it on.

Dana watched as her dear friend came out of the fitting room moments later. The gown was long and elegant, it had a style similar to her gown, in that they shared an empire waist and were gathered beneath the breasts. It was unique in its bead work both along the y neck detailing and the waist.

"It's a perfect complement. Look at us; we could be sisters," Dana said with a giggle. "Do you like it?"

"I love it and I should be able to wear it again later. When my sister got married, the gown she gave me was one that was so fancy it can never be used again," Gena stated.

"We'll take them both, thank you so much," Dana gushed with excitement. She had a dress and so did Gena, from there on it would be easy or so she'd been told. She wished for a moment that her Mom had been free to be there today but understood why she couldn't. "We have to take pictures first though, Mom will kill me if she doesn't get to see this."

"Right nearly forgot," Gena stated as she crossed the floor to her purse and dug out the camera. She snapped a few photos of Dana from various angles and then the sales woman took a couple of them together. The trio moved on to the jewelry display to have a peek and then after arranging an appointment for their alterations and first fittings left the shop and headed on to their next stop.

42

Dana sighed as she sunk down into Gena's love seat. She was tired from a long busy day. After finishing up at the bridal shop the pair had moved on to a couple different shoe stores looking for just the right pair. From there it had been a quick lunch before stopping in at the florist to discuss flowers. Their last stop of the day had been a video store for a new flick during their girls' night in.

"Man my feet are killing me. I'm so glad I went with something other than the shoes at the bridal shop." Dana stated.

"Yeah those things are not gentle on your feet at all. I learned that the hard way for my sister's wedding, besides the shoes you bought look better with your dress."

"Yep they do. Thank you for letting me keep everything here. Lance is so sneaky he'd have poked around looking for it at my place."

Gena laughed. "He's a cop, he doesn't like mysteries, it's to be expected."

"I know," Dana said with a yawn.

"You look wiped, are you sure you want to watch this now we can save it for tomorrow," Gena offered.

"I'm sure. If I crash now I'll be up at some hellish hour in the morning. Just a little tired from an early morning today."

"I thought you had the day off?"

"I did it was an early AM call. We got tagged because it was connected to our case."

"That Fury thing I've been reading about?"

"Yeah," Dana said with a sigh.

"I'm sorry, you sure you don't want to rest?"

"Positive, come on let's get this movie started."

Gena nodded and stuck the movie in her blue ray player. She flipped on the TV and pressed play. Dana stretched out on the couch as Gena put her feet up in the recliner and together the pair fell silent as they fell into the movie.

Lance sat sipping his coffee working on paperwork and trying not to look at the clock. Dana was late and it was driving him crazy. He'd never anticipated how much not having her around for a few days would affect him. He hadn't slept much since Sunday. Work had been tedious and home had been dull without her. He couldn't remember the last time he was this anxious for something. He wondered how he'd endure being without her the night before their wedding and tried not to think about it.

As he finished the last of his report the familiar sound of her heels clicking on the floor caught his ear and he smiled. Lifting his head he watched as she crossed the floor to their shared office. He drew a breath at the sight of her. She was a vision and if it was possible she looked better than before, there was a glow about her, something distinctly female. Lance wrapped his arms around her in a bear hug before kissing her until she was breathless.

"It's good to see you Dana. How was your break?" he questioned as he took his seat.

"It was frustrating, and wonderful. I found my dress only took two hours and then we moved on for shoes and lunch and flowers – it's going to be amazing I can't wait for you to see the flowers and the invitations. Mom say's hi by the way."

Lance laughed he'd never seen Dana so enthused. "Well for what it is worth I'm glad your back, I missed you," he stated.

"I missed you too, thank you for giving me a few days with Gena and Mom to get things moving."

"You're welcome. Not too much else of interest happened around here while you were gone our killer has gone silent not sure why."

"Maybe he's still looking for a new victim I mean since the report ran Monday people are being more careful," Dana stated.

"It's possible," Lance agreed, though he doubted it. Everything about their killer suggested he was well organized. He'd have already picked his next victim by now, something had happened to deviate him from plan. As he closed out the case file his email flashed indicating an incoming message.

Lance opened his email message box and noted a new message from an unknown account and cursed. "Looks like I spoke too soon," Lance grumbled as he clicked on the link knowing it was from their unknown subject of investigation. Just like the ones before it held a photo of the last victim with a warning beneath it.

I have located my next fury the time of her transformation draws near. The clock is ticking. Catch me if you can.

44

HE made his way up the short walk to her front door, the full moon looked down upon him as the blade in his coat hummed with excitement. He felt a prick of fear that heightened his pleasure, this one was different than the others before her, she was special a gift to the angel who pursued him with such passion.

"Dana," he breathed her name like a prayer as he slipped inside the darkened apartment using the hide-a-key in the rose bush. Within his coat the blade he carried warned him not to lose focus. Dana was not his target and he needed to stay the path ahead of him so that that which he desired the most would be his. The detective was a distraction she was not HIS SERENITY.

HE closed the door with care not to make too much noise. The apartment was dark and silent as a tomb. Nothing stirred – his new fury slept peacefully down the hall unaware of his presence. Despite her awareness of a danger in the city, she had not been able to pick up on him following her. HE'D been watching her for days now. HE knew her habits inside and out. She was lovely his fury and HE looked forward to initial contact.

As HE crept down the hall HE wondered if she'd wake when HE looked at her in her sleep as the woman before her had. Those bewitching hazel eyes had opened and gone wide with fear a moment before HE'D covered her face with the chloroform soaked rag preventing her from screaming. HE hoped this new one would wake as well his flesh burned with anticipation as HE slipped into her room.

On cat like feet HE crossed the room to her bed -side and stared down upon her sleeping form. She lay curled on her side half covered by the cool Egyptian cotton sheets. Her milk white skin exposed for him to see. HE studied her naked form with both awe and disgust as HE wondered if HIS SERENITY would sleep so. The knife told him it didn't matter for now, she was his fury not Serenity. She stirred in her repose kicking aside the sheet completely leaving nothing left for his imagination to fill in and his groin tightened at the sight of her. Undone HE crept to the other side of her bed and slipped in behind her with trembling fingers HE reached out to touch. She did not stir, simply purred under his gentle touch. Emboldened HE drew her back against him pressing his need against her bare skin.

She jolted awake fear radiated from her as reality came crashing in. She tore at his arm about her and hazel eyes wheeled in her skull trying to see who held her. Her lips parted to scream a moment too late as HE covered her lips and nose with the rag. As she went under HE whispered the name of the woman he craved in her ear allowing himself for a moment to believe HE held her close to him.

When HE was sure she was unconscious HE set his token for the detective to find after they identified the body, then wrapped the sheet about her and lifted her from the bed. With care HE carried her from her home and outside to his car. HE lay her gently in the back seat in the manor which a loving father might place his cherished child and closed the door with care not to jostle her before he climbed in the drives seat and drove off headed back for his lair.

45

Dana cursed as Lance pulled up along the perimeter of the park entrance. She could already see the yellow crime scene tape in the distance. Victim number four had been found a short time earlier by a morning jogger. The PD had been called immediately. She and Lance had been shaken from sleep only thirty minutes earlier. The warm cup of coffee in her hands did nothing to ease the chill that had settled in her bones upon waking. Something was wrong here she couldn't shake the feeling that whatever lay ahead of her in the park would alter the course of her life somehow.

She drew an uneasy breath and with trepidation pushed open her car door.

"You okay sweetie?" Lance questioned picking up on her mood.

"Yeah, just got a bad feeling about this one," she muttered as they crossed the street and walked into the park in the direction of the yellow tape. Danna spotted the angel first, it sat perched upon the top of the fountain. "That makes four she muttered and made a mental note to add a search for angelic figures to her possible crime scenes data.

Dana turned moving her attention onto where the coroner was busy at work. She blinked with muted disbelief as the lifeless pain filled eyes that met hers came into focus. Lance drew her face against his chest turning her gaze away from the grizzly sight of Gena broken and bleeding body. She pushed back tears and choked back a scream.

"He's been following you," Lance stated with disgust.

Dana pushed away from his embrace and the shield he offered. If the killer was following her then he was most likely watching them even now and she would not let him see her break. Instead she pulled herself together. Do the job, she demanded herself. "Yeah he may be watching even now. Officer please scout the area for anyone lingering that is non-police personnel or a witness."

The young black and white nodded then turned and walked off to do as she instructed. Dana slipped on a pair of gloves and stepped into the booties to cover her shoes before crossing under the crime scene tape to begin the investigation.

Like the others before her Gena's red hair had been cut short in the front to accommodate the golden crown of serpents set upon her brow. Beneath her eyes the skin had been cut open so that it appeared she wept tears of blood. Her body was draped in a crimson chiffon gown like the others, the style was distinctly Grecian. Her left breast lay exposed, a golden snake wrapped around her body its' fangs sunk into her flesh piercing her heart. At her side another serpent coiled about her right arm from elbow to wrist, its teeth sunk deep in the pulse point. A third gold band wound around her right leg from ankle to calf.

"It's definitely our guy, this is my fault. I felt like I was being watched when I left the station but I didn't see anything so I dismissed my instincts."

"Don't – this is not your fault, Dana. It's his! If it hadn't been Gena now, then down the line he still might have found her on his own. You didn't do this. He did." Lance stated.

Dana nodded acknowledging his words. She said nothing more as they went through the rest of the investigation work at the park.

46

Lance sat in a chair in the back of the funeral home alone, his blue eyes fixed on Dana. She stood up front behind the casket at a mike. He worried over the dark circles under her eyes her makeup was unable to hide and the thinness of her frame in her black pants suit. She'd lost weight since the last time he'd seen her. Dana had withdrawn from him since they found Gena in the park, she'd spent more time at her place than his now. They met only at work and only when their paths crossed due to the case. It was the first time he'd really seen her in weeks. She looked weary and sad as she began to speak.

"Gena Andrews was my dearest friend. She was full of joy and energy. She was a free spirit with an adventure's love of travel. Loyal and true, Gena had a kind heart that gave without asking anything in return. She was cut down by a senseless act of violence. To her family and friends and even to Gena herself if she is listening I swear to you that this crime will not go unsolved I will see to it the man responsible for this tragedy is brought to justice. He will pay for what he's done." Dana stated before she walked away from the mike.

Lance looked on with sympathy his heart breaking as she paid her final respects to her fallen friend and Gena's parents. She then made her way back to the empty chair beside him. Lance wrapped an arm around her shoulders and rubbed her back as she let her tears fall silently as others took their turns talking of the woman who lay still and lifeless in the closed casket. He brushed a kiss on her temple and whispered words of comfort in an attempt to ease her pain.

As the funeral drew to it's end he led his broken fiancé from the funeral home and out into the evening air. "Stay with me tonight Dana, please you shouldn't be alone." he requested.

She laid her head on his shoulder and allowed him to take her to his car. He opened the passenger door for her and helped her into her seat fastening her in and closing the door before rounding the vehicle to the driver's side and getting in. He drove across town to his place and led her inside locking the door behind them.

Once inside Lance settled Dana on the living room couch. He knelt down in front of her and slipped her heels off her feet. He switched on the TV before grabbing his phone and calling in an order of takeout food. As Dana sat in silence watching one of her favorite movies, Lance's mind ran over a mental checklist of things to do for her. First he was to get her to eat something even if it was soup, then he'd get her to take a long soothing shower or bath and finally he'd make sure she got a good night's sleep.

His bell rang a few moments later and Lance rose from his seat crossing to the front door. He took the food from the delivery guy paid him and then rejoined Dana in the living room. Lance set the bag of food on the coffee table and began to pull out its contents. He opened the container with the potato soup and let its tasty aroma fill the air.

"I think we should both eat something," Lance stated as he poured half the soup into a bowl for her. He watched as Dana blinked.

"Yeah, right," She answered as if her mind had come back from wandering elsewhere. She took the offered bowl and a spoon and began to eat. Lance ate his own soup in the eerie stillness that had settled between them. They'd never shared a meal without conversation. It scared him this quiet she had surrounded herself with. Only the movie prevented the room from being utterly silent.

To his relief she finished the soup and ate the rest of the meal he'd ordered. "Would you prefer a shower or a bath?" Lance asked.

"A bath," she replied after some thought.

Lance nodded and then rose from his seat, clearing their dishes before moving onto the bathroom to draw a tub of hot water. When it was ready he called for her. She joined him moments later.

"Thank you," she whispered before brushing a kiss on his lips.

Lance took her hand in his and kissed it. "You're welcome – I'll be in the bedroom if you need anything," he murmured before letting her go and leaving her to soak in privacy.

47

Dana stepped out of the tub dried off her skin before slipping into the PJ's Lance had left for her. She pushed back tears as she reflected on his tender care that day with her. He really was a great guy. She wondered how she'd been so lucky to find him as she thought of all the cases that came across her desk over the years that showed the horror of what men and women alike could do to one another.

She sighed as she let the water out of the tub; her thoughts turning again to Gena. She'd failed there and because of it a woman she considered like a sister had been put in the ground. God her heart ached with the truth of it. Though her parents and Lance had assured her she wasn't to blame Dana couldn't help but feel guilty. Turning she studied herself in the mirror. No wonder Lance looked so concerned. Dark circles had settled in under her brown eyes from countless nights she'd gone with little to no sleep. Her brown eyes seemed hollow and empty, the spark of life gone from them.

Dana wondered how long it had been since she'd eaten a real meal as she noted her face looked thinner. Her PJ's hung lower on her frame as well. She'd lost weight. She turned her gaze from the image in the glass. Picking up the brush she busied herself with straightening out her hair and turned her thoughts back to the case avoiding the decision she'd reached while lying in the tub, it would wait until morning.

Once she was done Dana moved into the bedroom and slipped into the bed. She felt Lance tuck her in and whispered a thank you before mumbling goodnight. The last thing she heard was Lance move into the bathroom probably to straighten it, then the sounds of his feet as he crossed back to the bed. She felt the mattress sink as he settled in next to her; the warmth of his skin as he drew her back against his chest. She sank into his embrace needing him to chase away the chill if only for the night.

48

Lance's eyes opened as the first hint of light began to peak through the curtains over his window. He glanced at the clock and noted the time. He was glad to find Dana still sleeping in his arms. Lance drew a breath and sighed they'd gotten through Gena's funeral together and they'd get through the case as well. He just needed her to let him help her as she'd done last night.

Awake and ready to start the new day Lance brushed a kiss on Dana's forehead and whispered a "sleep well," before slipping out of the bed and pulling on a clean shirt. He crept out of the room and made his way down the hall to the kitchen. Opening the fridge he pulled out the eggs, bacon, strawberries, yogurt, bagels and other various food items to prep breakfast. He pulled the skillet out and set it on the stove top then opened a drawer and pulled out a paring knife, and basic silverware.

Lance crossed the kitchen and opening other cabinets collecting bowls and plates. His materials gathered he moved back to the stove and began the process of preparing breakfast for himself and Dana, he'd surprise her with breakfast in bed and then they'd talk about the road ahead. He'd missed talking to her – missed her, he realized as he spooned yogurt into a bowl. Lance pulled out his jar of cinnamon and shook a good bit into it then crossed to the sink. He washed off the strawberries and other fruit he pulled out and began cutting it up. He tossed a couple handfuls of strawberries and blueberries in the yogurt and stirred up the mix.

Lance covered the dish with plastic wrap and set it in the fridge he then threw the rest of the fruit together in a bowl returning it to the fridge as well. With step one complete he turned his focus to prepping the vegetables for the omelets. He was cutting up a pepper when he felt he was no longer alone.

"Morning sweetie, how did you sleep? I was going to bring you breakfast in bed but since you're up you can help yourself. I've got your yogurt stuff in the fridge and some fresh fruit."

Silence answered him at first then sniffling. Concerned Lance turned his head to see what was wrong. Dana stood behind him tears in her eyes dressed for work her purse hung over her shoulder. Lance cursed to see her hurting. His rhythm thrown off he missed the vegetable he was still chopping up and sliced the tip of his finger.

"Shit!" Lance set down the knife and wrapped paper towel around the injured digit. "I'm sorry Dana I shouldn't have left you alone," he said feeling guilty. He crossed the floor to embrace her but she held up a hand to stop him.

"Don't you didn't do anything wrong you've been wonderful, but I can't stay here with you Lance." She stated as she lowered her hand.

"What? Why not?" Lance questioned both hurt and alarmed. It was then he noted the suit case in her other hand. He felt his stomach clench his heart skipped a beat. What was going on?

"I made a promise to Gena and her loved ones to find her killer and I meant it."

"I know you did sweetie and I'm going to help you. We'll figure it out together."

"No, I can't do that. I love you Lance, so much it blinds me. Because I was so preoccupied with wedding plans that psycho was able to get to my best friend. I can't be distracted like that again – I won't. I'm sorry but I can't do this anymore." Dana said. She drew the engagement ring off her finger and set it in his hand.

Lance was dumbfounded by her words and felt his world shift. He reeled, shaken to the core. His heart which had been still a moment ago now pounded wildly as fear took hold of him. His mouth went dry. It felt like a desert and as he opened his lips to speak his tongue felt too thick. He blinked trying to recover from what felt like a knockout blow. She wasn't just going to walk away without a fight. "Dana, please… don't do this honey. Gena wouldn't want this," Lance argued hoping to reason with her.

"I'm sorry," she murmured before she turned and fled. Lance hurried after her. When she tried to open the door he leaned against it stopping her.

"Dana, listen to me don't do this, your upset and over reacting. You're not thinking clearly. This isn't your fault baby."

"Yes it is. I led that monster to her. I could feel him watching but rather than really look for him when I didn't see anything I dismissed my instincts because I was too wrapped up in my own little world. I killed my best friend and I won't risk anyone else!"

"Sweetie, please, you know that these guys target single women. What's to stop him from coming after you?" Lance's mind caught up with what she had in mind and he felt his stomach churn with disgust. "Damn it Dana this isn't a game! You could get yourself killed setting yourself out as bait."

"I've thought long and hard about this and I could save other innocent women from his madness. It's a risk I'm willing to take if it will bring Gena's killer to justice."

"I won't let you do this I'll speak to the chief and stop it before you can even attempt it. I won't watch you destroy yourself because of an obsession."

"You can't stop me from doing this I'll do it on my own if I have to."

"I could have you arrested for your own protection." Lance threatened.

"Let me go Lance, I don't have anything left for you." She breathed as a horn honked outside.

Shaken by the sound, his grip on the door eased, he watched with disbelief as she hurried outside to a waiting cab. He called her name but she gave no response as if she hadn't heard him. He considered giving chase but knew it would be fruitless. There would be another day to try again. Lance looked down at his hand still pressed against the door and saw his own blood seeping from his makeshift bandage. Blood and death, his life day in and day out was filled with both, maybe it was time he changed that.

If he wasn't careful he knew despite his words he'd follow Dana every step of the way into her madness. He'd lose himself to the job. Lance wasn't about to let that happen. He was done with chasing psycho killers and wading through the darkest places of men's souls. He'd talk to the chief as he'd said and when he did he'd request a transfer.

He was done with homicide.

PART 5

SERENITY RISING

49

Catharine sat at the ornate, oblong, dark wood, antique writing desk provided by the hotel. The narrow desk had been her work space for weeks, while adequate it was not her private workspace. Here she was almost afraid to get to comfortable as her work space was generally a mess and this setting was too nice to make messy. She'd been without a space of her own for well over a month and she hoped this state of transition from one life to the other would come to an end soon. Catharine had applied the day before for a penthouse apartment overlooking Central Park. Maybe soon she'd be sitting at a desk of her own but for now the hotel was home and its beautiful antique desk currently held her most valuable possession, a sleek black laptop she'd scrimped and saved for; buying it with her own money when she first moved to New York. At the time she'd had plans to use it at school as she endeavored to pursue a law degree. Boy, did things change, she mused.

Beside the laptop sat old news clipping from a DC paper dated a few days earlier. The article written by Pamela Walsh discussed information pertaining to a bizarre string of murders in the DC area. The strange calling cards left by the killer from the golden snake bands to the bloody tears had captured Catharine's interest. The fact that the victims shared her appearance had only added fuel to an already over active imagination. Given her troubled past, at first, she'd wondered if perhaps Kurt had found her despite her care to remain hidden but according to the article the killer was left handed and Kurt was not.

Catharine shoved thoughts of Kurt aside, she'd closed that chapter of her life long ago just as she'd now sealed the book with Tom. She sighed as her blue eyes drifted down to the gold band still on her left ring finger. Though her divorce had been finalized months ago she still wore her wedding ring. Not because she missed Tom or had any regrets in ending their marriage but as a reminder to not get involved with a man again. She'd chosen badly twice, she wasn't about to try again right now and wind up in another nightmare at least for the present she'd be content to simply write of love.

Blue eyes moved away from the thin gold band to the screen of her computer. She glanced over her notes and made sure she was familiar with her character before opening a new file. Fingers moved to rest on the keys and moments later she was lost in the rhythmic sound of the keys as she pressed each one. Forming words and sentences on the electronic page as she shaped the stage for her newest work; as the scene began to take shape she felt a heavy weight lift from her shoulders. She was finally working on something other than Dark Heart. In a matter of months it would become a thing of the past and she'd be free of Serenity.

This was not the first time Catharine had written a book. It was actually her fourth novel in five years but it felt like the most important one to date. She'd written the first book Heart of Glass simply to try and free her mind of excess baggage from her life with Kurt. She had hoped that if she'd gotten it out of her head that it would have helped her marriage with Tom. Catharine had never intended for it to see the light of day but Tom's Mother had read it and loved it. She'd pressed her son to get it published and Tom had delivered. She wasn't sure of the particulars even now nor did she really care to learn just how her ex had sold the book but once the deal was made and the book had proved successful she'd been approached to do a second one.

Heart of Clay had been the result and Heart of Stone had followed soon after. Serenity had become an overnight sensation, everyone loved her; everyone except Catharine. Serenity was a weak willed girl and a constant reminder of a past she'd have preferred to forget. With a little luck all the interest in Serenity would die down after she introduced her fans to Jade.

Jade was her new heroine, a strong, smart and sexy reporter who would be targeted by the dangerous killer and manage to escape. Her path would cross that of a detective whom she would end up getting involved with during the time in which he was protecting her from the crazed killer. During the story they'd manage to catch the killer save the day and fall in love. It was just the sort of thing romance readers loved and if she could add a fantasy element to it all the better as her current fans seemed to like that element in the Dark Heart Series. With the new novel she was hoping to cross the bridge from mainstream romance to mystery or thriller. She didn't want CJ

Nichols to become synonymous with Dark Erotic Fantasy.

Pushing these thoughts aside Catharine lost herself in the scene. The shrill call of the room phone drew her back to reality hours later. She blinked as she rose from the table and crossed to the bed.

"Hello," she questioned as she cradled the phone between her shoulder and her face. Glancing at the clock she noted it was nearly noon. A good start, though she'd have preferred to not been interrupted. One of the draw backs of living at a hotel, it wasn't so easy to close out the rest of the world here as it was in your own home.

"Good afternoon Catharine, how are you doing today?" A familiar male voice asked.

"Bryan, things are going well here I've got a good start on the new book."

"That's great. I'm sorry to disturb you while you're working, but it can't be helped. We need to meet,"

"What's up?"

"Big news. Can you be down in the Peacock Room in fifteen?"

"I guess. Can we go somewhere less crowded? I'd rather avoid the fans."

"Sorry CJ not today see you in fifteen minutes," Bryan answered and before she could ask any additional questions he hung up. Catharine sighed and blew her red bangs out of her face annoyed. She'd need to get dressed as her PJs would not suit for a public meet. So much for her lazy day; Catharine saved her file and then closed the laptop. She crossed over to the closet, pulled out her favorite suit then moved into the bathroom to get ready.

50

Catharine stepped off the elevator and into the lobby of the Waldorf Towers, the luxurious space had not been her idea for a place to land while she worked to find herself a new home in the Big Apple. Catharine had planned on staying at a Holiday Inn or someplace less public, she'd never been one to seek the finer things in life. Her publicist had insisted. She was after all a big name in the writing world and she could afford to indulge he'd stated, besides if the press got wind she was in town it would be better for her image to be seen in this setting. The marble floors and fancy upscale furnishings would just add further prestige to CJ Nichols name and make her fans desire to get lost in her world all the stronger.

Catharine laughed if they only knew that behind all the glitz and glamour of her stage was a newly divorced woman with no romantic experience what so ever in her past, they might not rush to dive in her world so quickly. It was ironic really that given her track record she could even write about romance. As Catharine made her way through the lobby toward the Peacock Room she was relieved to find few patrons in the area. With a little luck she'd not be spotted and could join Bryan in peace.

Any hopes of avoiding an unwanted conversation were dashed as a young woman with blond hair and stunning blue eyes squealed with excitement as she spotted her.

"Oh my, it is you, I thought so. CJ I am such a huge fan. I saw you in Vegas during your first book tour. I'm Ellen."

"Hello Ellen it's nice to meet you," Catharine said politely she hoped this wouldn't draw others to gather.

"I'm just so excited. I love Serenity, she's like the greatest heroine ever. I don't suppose you could sign my book. I never go anywhere without it. I've read the trilogy a million times."

"I'd be happy to," Catharine said simply and listened as Ellen gushed on about her love of Serenity and the series.

"I have a question will you be writing another book, I mean what about her happy ending. You're not going to leave her alone forever are you?" Ellen questioned as she handed over a well-worn copy of the paperbacks.

"I don't have any plans to write another Dark Heart novel. Unfortunately, Serenity has become a vampire and as you know in my world they are all evil she'd have to be the villain in a fourth book." Catharine took the books and with a pen signed each.

"You could make her an anti-hero out for revenge against the vampires…"

"Yes I could, but it would not make for a very romantic tale. There are no plans for another story with Serenity I've recently started a new project and am contracted to deliver that title at the beginning of next year." Catharine stated as she handed back the novels.

"Oh, well maybe when you're done?" Ellen asked with hope in her eyes.

"Maybe, Catharine relented recalling what Bryan had said about not dashing their hopes. I'm sorry, but I need to go I'm meeting with my publicist."

"Oh, okay I understand, maybe we'll run into each other again and can talk more," Ellen asked.

"Perhaps, it was nice meeting you Ellen," Catharine said politely, then she turned and went on her way praying that the rest of her walk would be uninterrupted.

51

Bryan watched with interest and amusement as CJ handled her fan. The woman he knew as Catharine was a stunning beauty with long red hair and vivid blue eyes that hit like a shock to the system when she looked at you. He'd tried for years to convince her to place her portrait on the back cover of her novels knowing that if she were seen it would increase her sales but Catharine refused to do so. For reasons she'd yet to reveal CJ preferred to remain hidden from the public eye. He'd figured that when she split from Tom that her objections to running the photo would have eased but instead they'd increased.

As she turned from the young blonde Bryan wondered what his writer was hiding from but knew enough about her not to ask. Catharine was a private and secretive woman and when pushed to reveal her life, clammed up. It had taken years after meeting her to get her to talk about her life with Tom; to earn her trust. Bryan figured given time she'd tell him all. He watched as a pair of sexy legs strolled across the rest of the lobby, high heels clicking on the marble floor. He loved to watch her move, grace and fluidity defined her; each step was poetry. No movement made was wasted.

He noted she was wearing her favorite suit, a beautiful blue blazer with a purple silk blouse and a green pencil skirt with a peacock feather pattern. Bryan smiled, it seemed his favorite writer was in good spirits this morning. He hoped his news for her would be received well. Bryan felt those baby blues settle on him and waved. Her strides changed becoming long and quick eating up the distance between them. Bryan sighed, so much for her good mood. He knew the walk well and knew it signaled temper.

Bryan smiled and watched as she slid into the booth opposite him. "Good morning CJ," he said politely as she picked up her menu and began to look it over.

"Morning Bryan," she answered civilly and he knew he was in for an unpleasant meet.

"What's up sweetie," he questioned trying to cut right to the problem and get her back on an even keel.

"I wish you could have picked a different location for this little meet, I really don't want to deal with my fans today." She admitted.

"Sorry for the public venue but I suggest you get used to the fuss."

"Why?"

"Heart of Glass was optioned for film this morning."

"It was?" Catharine questioned with shock and disbelief.

"Yeah, James Hardagen put in a bid to put it on the big screen. Smile girl, Serenity is going to join a number of other heroines of late from novels to make the jump to motion picture."

"Wow," Catharine said with a bit of enthusiasm.

"Yeah you did it CJ. You've officially made the big show. You're due out in LA tomorrow to meet with him and start work on the script."

"That soon? I just started work on my new project I was hoping to dig in…"

"Well, it'll keep. Our top priority right now is the script also the publishing house wants to set up some kind of contest giveaway for the fans to drum up sales for the trilogy again. They think the series should draw new readers again and they want to strike while the irons hot. So start thinking about a possible prize package for a vacation getaway."

"Okay. What about my apartment here? I'm supposed to hear about closing this week?" Catharine said alarmed.

"Don't worry CJ I'll handle that; you just get yourself packed and I've got you out on the first flight to LA." Bryan assured her.

Catharine nodded.

"Good now I think a toast is in order," Bryan said and the waiter came to the table with a bottle of champagne. He poured two flutes and handed them over to Bryan before he withdrew. "To Serenity," Bryan said as he raised his glass.

"To a movie," Catharine answered before she sipped from her glass. Bryan watched as his favorite author's body language eased and knew that her mood had shifted again she was now at ease and it made him happy. The pair finished their drinks and then after a brief discussion of her itinerary for her flight CJ rose from her seat, brushed a kiss on his cheek then turned and headed back for her hotel room.

Bryan sat in his booth a few moments more watching as she went. His brown eyes fixed on the swing of her hair with each step. His focus moved on, drawn to the sexy sway of her hips and he smiled for a moment pleased. It was shaping up to be a good day and with Tom out of the picture it might just turn into his year.

52 LOS ANGELES, CALIFORNIA
TUESDAY
9PM

Catharine made her way down the escalator in LAX, when she reached the lower level she sighed at the sight of a driver with a sign for CJ Nichols, along with reporters waiting. The circus was already beginning and she'd only been in town for five minutes. Lucky for her Miss Nichol's appearance was not common knowledge. She'd just head over to the baggage claim get her things and slip out unnoticed. A cab would be more than good enough to get her to the hotel and on to the studio in the morning. Catharine reasoned.

Any thoughts of slipping out unnoticed died when the driver locked eyes with her and waved her over. Catharine cursed apparently he'd been notified in advance of who to look for. A moment later the camera's turned to point at her.

"Miss Nichols is it true you're in negotiations to turn Heart of Glass into a film?" a thin and sexy brunette questioned holding her mike out.

"No comment," Catharine replied as she walked past the woman and the camera man toward the silent driver. "Move," she instructed as she moved past him in the direction of the baggage claim.

"CJ is there any truth to the rumors flying around in New York that you and your publicist have moved from just friends to something more?"

Catharine froze mid stride shocked by the question, she'd heard nothing about speculation surrounding her or Bryan. "There is no truth to such claims at all." Catharine answered coolly before grabbing her bag. She then turned and locked eyes with the troublesome reporter. "We're done here. You'll be notified about any developments here in town regarding Dark Heart when the rest of the press is."

"Of course."

"Off the record legs if I see you again before then I'll have a restraining order filed. I don't do public appearances outside book signings, you should know that. Local press in New York understands I value my space I suggest you learn the same or I'll have you knocked down to celeb obituaries."

"Why is it that you're so secretive Miss Nichols?"

"Are we still off the record?"

The reporter nodded.

"Survival." Catharine muttered, before she vanished into the crowd once more an anonymous figure.

"Survival?" The reporter questioned with interest as she watched the writer vanish. She turned her attention to her notes and sighed. The name she'd recently learned that went with Nichols was Catharine Jade, only trouble was when she'd looked into the name she'd found it was a fake. So who was the real CJ Nichols and who was she hiding from.

53

Catharine sat in the back seat of the black sedan trying to shake off the encounter with the reporter. It was getting worse now that Dark Heart had hit big. She was getting pressure from the house to add a photo to the book jacket now that she and Tom were over. They assumed that her need to remain a faceless writer was over. They were wrong. She'd not told anyone not even Bryan that Tom was not the reason for her refusal to add a photo to the book cover. Tom was not her monster hiding in the dark. He was just a minor annoyance. No, CJ Nichols would remain a name without a face because she didn't dare risk being recognized. The woman she'd once been was dead and Catharine was not about to let her ghosts come back to haunt her.

Her decision made Catharine pulled a beer out of the mini fridge and twisted off the cap. She took a gulp of the cool suds and let the alcohol work its magic to calm her nerves as she closed the book on her past once more. As the sedan pulled to a stop; Catharine set aside her empty bottle once more at ease. She slipped out of the studio car and followed her driver across the studio lot to the sound stage where James Hardagen sat behind a desk waiting.

Catharine watched as his blue eyes lit with enthusiasm and he rose from his seat.

"CJ it's a pleasure to meet you." He said with his signature smile as he offered her his hand.

"Mr. Hardagen," she answered politely before shaking his hand.

"All business, I see the rumors are true then."

"Afraid so, so what made you decide to pick Dark Heart for your big come back?"

"I was blown away by the characters after reading it. There's so much there that will translate well to the big screen."

"Thank you, but before I agree to write a script for you James, I need you to understand that this can't become a love letter to Serenity's fans I want it to stay true to my vision and the world which I've created."

"Of course, I want this done right CJ that's why I requested you on the script." James assured her.

"Okay I'll get started on an outline as soon as I get back to the hotel. The house wants to put together a contest give away to drum up interest again. I'll let you know what we put together there as well; hopefully tie it to the film as well."

"Sounds good. How soon can I expect a script?"

"I'll have the outline for you in 24hrs. If you approve I'll start work on the script tomorrow night."

"Great."

"I'll require a voice in the selection of the actress who plays Serenity at least as she is the heart and soul of this project. If we get the right one for her, the rest will fall in place."

"Fair enough I'll want a script for book two and three as well. I'm planning on doing the other two if I can prove the first will do well."

Catharine nodded speechless. It was to be expected she told herself but it was more than she'd ever dreamed of when she first penned Heart of Glass. "That shouldn't be a problem. I'll see you tomorrow Mr. Hardagen." Catharine stated before she turned and headed back out to the car. She couldn't wait to get started, maybe this would give her the opportunity to make the changes to the book series she'd wanted to but until now had been unable to. Film adaptation gave her the freedom to take the book where she intended without the house looking over her shoulder. Seeing the chance to close the book on Serenity for good Catharine smiled as she got back in the sedan. It was going to be a long night but with a little luck when she was done she'd be free of Serenity forever.

54

As Catharine rode across town she turned her thoughts from the script to the contest the house wanted to create. How could she capture the romance, of a story she hated, for others to enjoy. She supposed the easiest solution would be to send them on a getaway trip for two to Greece since that was where she had set the Dark Heart trilogy but reasoned the publishing house would not want to spring for the cost of round trip tickets, transportation upon arrival and lodging accommodations. So if that was out then what was her alternative?

She needed something that had the ambiance of ancient Greece in art and appearance but was not Greece. As she contemplated the matter her thoughts drifted back to her recent failed marriage and she sighed. What did she know about romance? Her latest attempt had proved to be a horrendous failure. Tom, how had she managed to misjudge him so immensely? Catharine combed her fingers through her red hair and tried not to wander too far down that mental track. She was done with it, she'd closed the book on Tom, he was no more.

Unbidden a conversation from before they got married popped into her head. Tom was telling her all about his big trip out to Vegas before they tied the knot. 'They've got everything out there a bit of Paris the pyramids and even Greco roman.' Catharine grinned that would work Caesar's Palace in Vegas would provide the setting for the romantic getaway she was looking for and yet not cost too much that the publishing house would balk at it. She could arrange for the winner to receive attire appropriate to the setting of the novel, a lovely Grecian gown and jewelry and during the getaway maybe have a celebration ball similar to one Serenity attends in Heart of Glass.

Yeah that would be perfect they could even have some of the films cast attend so that their winner could meet the Hollywood version of Serenity. It was brilliant not only would the fans love it they could sell tickets and books to other fans and still manage to take the spotlight off of her and place it on the real celebrities. She'd need some sort of prize to be given to the winner at the ball, also in keeping with the series but this was definitely in keeping with what Bryan was looking for, she couldn't wait to pass the idea on to him. With that done and the script moving forward nicely she'd have time to work on her new project on the side without anything else interfering.

Taking out her cell phone Catharine shot a quick text to her Publicist. "Got an idea for the contest."

A moment later she received Bryan's response. "Great what is it?"

Catharine sent him a short write up of what she'd put together in her head and sent it to him. She then stretched out in the back seat of the limo and yawned. It had been a long day but a good one. She managed to get quite a bit done for the script already and now so long as Bryan approved she had the contest nailed down fairly well also. All in all a good days work.

Her phone chirped signaling an incoming reply. She looked down to the screen and smiled. It seemed she'd nailed the contest idea out of the park, Bryan was ecstatic. As she skimmed over the reply she groaned at the comment about being out in the public eye again but had figured it would be coming.

"What about my new book? I'm still on deadline." Catharine sent in question as she considered the fact that when she reached the hotel her current transportation would attract a crowd. She wished that rather than the flashy ride she'd been given a studio car. She was not looking forward to the crowd that would gather at the hotel. Catharine preferred to stay out of the public eye. She knew that the publishing house was trying to connect her face with the name CJ. She really wished they'd just do as she asked and use a model or actress to put on the dust jacket and make her public appearances.

Catharine was not comfortable with the idea of her face being out in the world for anyone to see. There were people from her past she'd prefer to never run into again. Bryan meant well trying to get her in the spotlight, he was proud of her series wanted to see it and her career as a writer take off like a shooting star streaking across the heavens for all to see. Catharine wanted to be successful but not at the cost of her anonymity.

More than anything though she didn't want to be known only for Dark Heart; Serenity was not someone she was proud of. There were days she wished she'd never put pen to paper and written Heart of

Glass. No, that was inaccurate, there were days she wished she'd never let Tom's Mother read it.

The book was never meant to see the light of day. It had just been used as an outlet for all her pent up emotional baggage. Vivian had found it one night during a family gathering and started reading it. Catharine had been mortified but Vivian had been impressed, she'd begged to read the rest and Catharine had caved. Next thing she'd known she was getting a call from her mother-in-law telling her how the book was fabulous and she passed it on to a publisher friend of hers. The friend who was reading it soon informed Vivian she wanted it.

Over a peaceful dinner Vivian announced that Heart of Glass was being considered for publication and Catharine sputtered with disbelief, she'd mentioned Tom's career and that having a wife who wrote such stories might not be beneficial. Vivian had mentioned using a pen name and not putting her face on the book. Then told her not to worry about anything Tom would negotiate the sale. Before Catharine could protest any further it was done. Heart of Glass was sold and the Dark Heart trilogy began.

Her phone chirped once more signaling Bryan's reply. "Deadline has been extended focus on script."

"Okay will do." Catharine sent back before ending the discussion. She put her phone away then rubbed her temples a headache trying to form behind her eyes both at the implications of Bryan's reply and the memory. She pushed both matters aside and tried not to dwell too much on the matter; it was done. Dark Heart was complete and soon Serenity would fall by the wayside like every storybook character. The new piece would take the foreground and the mystery thriller she was looking to fashion would take center stage. CJ Nichols career as a dark fantasy romance novelist would come to a close and the mystery writer would step into the spotlight.

Catharine felt the limo slow down as they neared her destination.

"Can you just let me out here at the corner but drive over to the hotel? Maybe while the crowd is speculating over who you're picking up I can slip in unnoticed," Catharine requested.

"Yes Miss Nichols if you'd like I can bring something a little more inconspicuous tomorrow," the driver offered.

"That would be great. When should I expect you?"

"Around 9am I believe is when Mr. Hardagen requested for me to pick you up."

"Okay then I'll be sure I'm ready; night and thank you."

"Night Miss Nichols and welcome to LA," the driver said before he came to a stop at the red light. Catharine slipped out the back and walked the last block to the hotel. As planned he pulled up in front of the pickup area and the crowd gathered speculating who was getting out or who would be getting in. In the midst of the spectacle Catharine slipped in unnoticed.

55

Catharine stepped into the studio car her driver had selected and was pleased to find it was indeed nothing of note, the green Toyota 4-Runner did nothing to suggest anyone of importance rode inside.

"Where are we off to this morning?" Catharine questioned noting they were not pointed in the direction of the studio where she'd met Mr. Hardagen the day before.

"I take it your itinerary hasn't been handed down to you this morning?"

"No."

"Sorry to hear that, I'll make sure you get a copy with your wake up call. You've got a book signing gig."

"Perfect. How long?" Catharine asked exasperated. Bryan was going to pay for this.

"A couple hours."

"Right, okay then before we get there I'm going to need coffee."

"Consider it done Miss Nichols."

"You can call me CJ." Catharine offered not comfortable with being Miss it was just so proper."

"All right then CJ, where too?"

Catharine indicated her preferred place for coffee and they made the stop along the way. About thirty minutes later she was out of the 4 Runner and walking into the book store, her driver at her side.

"Security," he explained with a sheepish grin before leading her over to the table set up for her meet and greet with the fans. She took a seat behind the table beside the stack of Dark Heart novels.

Catharine sipped her coffee as her driver stood watch. "Hey I don't think we've been properly introduced yet since it seems we'll be seeing a lot of each other I can't keep thinking of you as the driver as you're clearly more than that," Catharine stated as she eyed her body guard, staff, what exactly was his job description title she wondered?

"Bill."

"Nice to meet you Bill, I'm Catharine," she said simply before turning her focus to the front doors as the manager opened the store for business.

The crowd of women that poured in, about made Catharine choke on her coffee. It was going to be a long morning.

56

Catharine sat once more in the back seat of the SUV on the move with Bill taking her to her next destination. She was grateful to be free of the crazed Serenity fans. She spent half the day signing copies of Dark Heart and fielding questions about Serenity and the possibility of a fourth book. She was exhausted and looking forward to a quiet lunch.

"What's next on the agenda for the day?" Catharine questioned.

"Lunch meeting with Mr. Hardagen and your publicist."

"Bryan's in town?" Catharine questioned with surprise.

"Yeah, I picked him up at the airport just before I came and got you for the book signing event."

"Oh, he didn't mention he was coming into town last night."

"Probably slipped his mind," Bill suggested.

"So, what is you official job title Bill," Catharine questioned her curiosity getting the better of her.

"Me, I guess I prefer to be called a transporter. You know like the movies I move valuable commodities for various employers and ensure they remain safe."

Catharine laughed at that. "Nice I like that it seems accurate and yet Hollywood vague." She commented as she made a mental note to include a transporter in her mystery novel it would make for an interesting secondary character to have either her hero or heroine interact with. "So, do you get to join us for lunch or are you taking a break."

"A break, Mr. Hardagen doesn't like to discuss business with staff around."

"Gotcha. Well then I'll see you later and I hope you enjoy your down time Bill." Catharine said before she stepped out of the SUV and made her way into the restaurant. If she got a moment alone with Bryan he was going to get an earful about the little stunt he'd pulled on her this morning. She preferred time to prepare for these public appearances. He knew that and had deliberately left her in the dark. He'd better have a damn good reason for it or else.

Upon entering the lobby she spotted the two men waiting at the bar. She crossed the room and joined them. Greeting Mr. Hardagen with a polite hello and then turning her attention to her publicist.

"Bryan what an unexpected surprise, I thought you were still in New York," she said evenly.

"I was but I had a couple things we need to discuss in person," he said. His smile was all charm the one he reserved for the publishing house or business contacts. Catharine hated it because she knew it was as fake, as his clip on tie.

"I see, so I guess that's why I didn't get any news about the book signing this morning?" Catharine asked pointedly.

"CJ sweetie I'm sorry about that it was a last minute thing no time to notify you, I literally got the call from the store after I got into town. I'm sorry for the lack of notice but it couldn't be helped they had to reschedule last minute their guest for today canceled last minute. We got bumped up."

"Okay but please in the future try to give me a heads up."

"Of course, so first I wanted to show both of you this," Bryan said with a flourish before presenting an 8 x10 glossy ad for the contest. The image was of a pail skinned beauty with golden hair, her blue eyes wide with fear and desire. Tears tracked down her cheeks. She was garbed in a Grecian toga of white. Her left arm is raised above her, embracing the neck of the man behind her. He is as white as chalk with golden hair. His blue eyes gleam with a hidden power. His arms are wrapped around her waist, drawing her back against him. His mouth is pressed at her throat his fangs sunk deep in her flesh. Blood runs down her skin to form letters.

Catharine's eyes skip over the writing taking in the rest of the image.

A cold stone tower lay directly behind them. A torch lit in the window reveals a pair of eyes the color of steel looking down upon them with hate and longing. The woman's other arm reaches towards the silhouette of a man in the foreground, who reaches back to her. Behind them to the left another man stands skin ruggedly tan, dark hair long and wild. His amber eyes, inhuman, stare at the woman with hunger. Above it all is a heart of glass it has shattered to look like the moon and stars in the night sky.

Catharine is impressed by the art work, it clearly captures the images at the core of the Dark Heart trilogy, foreshadowing

Serenity's troubled path she'll walk but not giving anything away. Turning her focus to the writing Catharine smiled, it seemed her idea had been given the green light. "Embrace the night. Enjoy a weekend getaway for two at Caesars Palace Hotel in Vegas. Magic awaits you at the Serenity Ball."

"Wow they put this together fast," she commented.

"Sounds like a great way to gain attention for both the book and the movie," Hardagen said pleased.

"Yeah we thought maybe that when this happens we could get a few cast members there for the ball, yourself perhaps as well." Bryan stated.

"Maybe, sounds good." Hardagen replied noncommittally.

"What was the other thing you needed to talk to me about?" Catharine questioned,

"You're application for the apartment off Central Park was accepted here are your keys." Bryan said with amusement as he handed her a set of keys.

"Oh, that's great news, no more hotel," she said pleased.

"I've made arrangements to have your stuff moved in before you get back. Congratulations CJ." He said before giving her a quick hug.

Catharine returned the brief embrace a little uneasy at the contact as it was outside their normal interaction but let it slide due to all the good news. As he let her go, the hostess joined them at the bar and informed them their table was ready. The trio followed after her, moving to claim their spot and enjoy their meal. With business covered they ate together in a companionable silence. Once they had finished their meals Mr. Hardagen had a bottle of Champaign brought over.

"To the rise of Serenity, may today's endeavor be the start of a long profitable relationship," he said with amusement as he lifted his glass in toast.

"To the movie," Catharine amended. She was not about to toast to Serenity's rising. If she had her way, Serenity would soon be nothing more than a passing phase in her career.

"To CJ," Bryan added and then the trio brought their glasses together and drank. The celebratory mood continued on and they'd soon polished off the bottle and were well on their way into a second when Catharine decided she needed to slow things down. She was a light weight when it came to drinking and the last thing she needed right now was to get herself wasted.

She ordered a desert and ate it as the two men continued to indulge in their drink. When she'd polished off her desert Catharine bid her associates good day stating she needed to get back to the script. Bryan gave her another quick hug and a light kiss on the cheek before she left. The exchange made her feel a bit uneasy. She hoped her publicist didn't have any ideas about picking up with her where Tom had left off. She was in no way interested in getting tangled up with a man again anytime soon. In the end she wrote it off to his being a little buzzed and let the matter go.

As Catharine slipped into the backseat of the 4 Runner she was glad for Bill because she knew she had no business driving.

"Where to CJ?"

"The hotel, Bill," she replied.

He nodded and pulled away from the curb. "Did you have a nice lunch?"

"Yeah it was pleasant enough," Catharine replied.

"That's good."

"How was your break?"

Bill smiled at her question and she noted he looked a bit surprised at her asking. "Nice grabbed lunch with the wife."

"Oh, that's sweet."

He laughed at her reply. "If it's not too much trouble, could you sign a copy of Heart of Clay for her? She loves Rachel and Derrick. When I told her I was transporting you she just beamed.

"Sure, no trouble at all."

"You're a nice lady CJ not many of my clients bother to talk with me let alone are willing to indulge my wife," Bill said speaking his mind.

"Thank you, I'm not really used to all this fuss," Catharine admitted.

"It shows but it's a good thing."

"Who do I make the book out to?"

"Jackie."

"Remind me to get it to you before I get back to the hotel," Catharine requested before she shut her eyes to rest.

"Will do," Bill assured her before falling silent allowing her to rest.

57

Upon arriving at the hotel Catharine took the paperback from Bill and noted that while clearly it had been read it was well cared for. Jackie it seemed was careful with her books and she imagined that Bill's wife would use the same care with anything she cherished. Opening the cover Catharine wrote a thoughtful inscription then signed it before handing the book back to her transporter.

"Thanks CJ she'll love this,"

"You're welcome Bill. She must be a lucky lady to have caught your eye," Catharine stated.

"Nah, I'm the lucky one," Bill corrected before she got out of the car and made her way up the stairs toward the lobby.

Once back in her hotel room Catharine sat down in front of her laptop and set to work on the script, she made mental notes of things she would change, writing changes that would bring an end to all the questions surrounding Serenity. When she was satisfied with her work she typed it out and saved it.

Her thoughts drifted to her transporter Bill and Jackie and her mood fell a little. That was what she had wanted with Tom, a loving devoted relationship of partners. What she'd gotten had been well, anything but. Catharine sighed as she closed out the file for Serenity, she was not going to dive too deep into it now when she was a little buzzed, she needed to focus on something else. Turning on her music she crossed to the mini fridge and pulled out a couple small bottles of vodka. Since she wasn't going anywhere else anytime soon she reasoned that she could stand for a little bit of a private celebration. She'd made it to the big show, granted not under the circumstances she'd hoped for but she was there none the less.

As she drank she assured herself it had nothing to do with her failed marriage or the sorrow she felt at knowing she was once more completely alone in this world. She didn't miss Tom or their life together she told herself but a part of her knew she was a liar. Every part of her life was as made up as the mystery novel she would soon write. Catharine 'CJ' Nichols was a fake. She wondered what would happen if that ever got out. She contemplated what the   ripples would look like if the truth ever came out and felt that old familiar fear creep in on her at the notion that HE might find her.

Catharine took another swig of vodka as she assured herself that couldn't happen. Figuring she'd had enough Catharine set her bottle aside and poured a cup of coffee. She then turned her attention back to her laptop. Opening the file labeled new project she read over her concept notes again, along with the news stories on the bizarre slayings in DC using the grim details to sober herself up. If she was ever going to be free of Dark Heart she had to finish her newest work then maybe she'd be remembered for something better than Serenity.

PART 6

THE ASSIGNMENT

58 Unknown

Sam Abrams woke to foreign surroundings. He was in a 10x10 concrete room laying on an uncomfortable, standard issue, small, prison cot.

Where was he?

How had he gotten there?

Sam searched his fuzzy mind and recalled walking through Potomac Park. He was waiting for his contact with information on Kadar Handel's location when someone bumped into him. He'd felt a jolt and then...

Nothing.

As he groaned, he determined that based on the cottony feel of his mouth that he'd been drugged during the bump. By whom he could only guess. Based on the lack of anything useful in his surroundings he figured that whoever had collected him knew well what he was capable of and didn't want to see him escape,

that implied either his employer or a well instructed enemy. Given he was not bound, Sam figured he'd been picked up by his employers.

As he sat up the door opened. "Mr. Abrams, this way," a man's voice commanded. Sam got to his feet and walked out of the holding cell. It seemed he'd soon learn the reason for his abduction.

59

Sam was lead down a narrow corridor lined with a half dozen iron doors whose only visible feature was a 2 x 3 glass window dead center. Peering in he noted it allowed for persons on the outside of the cell to view the individual being held.

The hall came to an end in front of a security door where his guard scanned a pass card before ushering him through. Each wall down the new passageway held a door. The one directly ahead of him required a card key and entry code for access, along with a hand print scan; by the look of the biometric plate next to the key pad.

Experience told Sam he was looking at the weapons depot and personal affects storage room for the Company. The two other rooms were interview suites.

Sam chuckled at the notion, that was just the agencies polite way of saying interrogation wing.

His escort used his card key to open the door on the right side of him and issued him in.

"Have a seat Mr. Abrams, he'll be in to speak with you momentarily," the man instructed before he walked out.

Sam sighed as he took a seat at the long stainless steel table in the cold, hard, matching chair. The room was like that of a prison visitation chamber except it lacked a ring for securing a prisoner's chains. He'd been in here before but on the other side of the table as the one conducting the interview, looking for answers. It seemed that now he would be the one questioned.

Sam supposed he should have seen this coming, after all he'd failed to complete his last assignment. He'd just hoped that a formal inquiry would not be necessary given the circumstances. As Sam prepared himself mentally for the battle he was about to wage the security door slid open and his superior stepped inside.

The older man had thinning salt and pepper hair that was cleanly cut. He wore a black suit with a white dress shirt and matching tie. In his hands he carried a leather portfolio.

The newcomer took a seat at the table opposite Sam and flipped open the leather bound report. His steel colored eyes turned directly to the file ignoring the subject of the meet. A pair of black rimmed glasses sat perched on the bridge of his nose but he was far from blind. Mr. Jones was as observant as any man half his age and sharper than most.

His eyes, skimmed over the report before lifting to meet with Sam. "Mr. Abrams, do you know why you are here today?"

"I would imagine it has something to do with my failure to complete my last assignment," Sam stated knowing it best to be direct and to the point with the older man. He didn't look kindly on excuses or finger pointing.

"That is correct. Not only did you lose your target Mr. Abrams you managed to completely blow your cover as well. My records indicate that the reason was a civilian is that accurate?"

"Yes sir, I was forced to let Kadar Handel escape in order to protect an innocent."

"I see. Well, one of your fellow agents has raised concerns that you're objectivity has been compromised. As a result you've been burned. Your employment with the Company is to be terminated. The job at the paper closed."

"Sir, I know I failed to complete my task but it's the first time this has happened. I'm asking you to please reconsider this matter. I'm a solid agent. My skills are above board and my loyalty undeniable."

"While I can appreciate what you are saying Abrams I'm afraid our recent evaluation suggests otherwise. Your loyalty is   divided now by this woman. If you truly wish to continue to work for us you'll have to leave, Miss Walsh."

"I can't do that sir, Pamela is my wife," Sam argued.

"Then Mr. Abrams we are done. Miss Walsh is a wild card we're not willing to risk."

"Sir…"

"I'm sorry son, your services are no longer needed," Mr. Jones said coolly before rising from his chair. "You'll need to turn over your passports, ID's, Credit cards, deposit box keys and any foreign currency you may still have in your possession as well as all weapons and gear."

Sam nodded his understanding.

"You're a good man Abrams I'm sorry to lose you," his employer added before he walked out of the interview suite.

Sam's handler returned a few moments later and issued him into the weapons depot where he turned over the required materials and filled out the necessary paperwork that would sever his ties for good with the Agency.

60

Sam moved through the underground parking garage connected to the main headquarters of a small DC newspaper that served as cover for the elite antiterrorist unit. He slipped behind the wheel of his Audi A8 and locked himself in.

How had it come to this? He asked himself trying to sort through the mess he was now in the center of.

The assignment he'd been given had been a relatively easy one by comparison to the previous one. Hell he'd even been back in the states after spending the last several years in the Middle East working with Israeli Masada. The company had been tracking the movements of a newly discovered terrorist cell. The only information they'd been able to glean to date was that the self-appointed leader of the shadow network was called Mr. York.

No one knew who he was or even what he looked like. Until about a year ago he didn't even exist except on paper. What they had learned after months of digging was that Mr. York was recruiting. He was sending out some sort of test mission to potential team members.

The Agency had intercepted a transmission to a former Iraqi mercenary Kadar Handel. It had been Sam's job to find Handel detain him and take his place. His ultimate end game was infiltrating Mr. York's unit and then tearing it down.

Locating Kadar had proved simple. The man had been hiding in DC working for a security company. Sam had been studying the man's movements for weeks. Looking for his best opportunity to complete; phase one. Kadar's routine changed with a phone call. Mr. York changed the man's assignment from an assassination to a robbery. The phone call Sam supposed, signaled the beginning of the end for his career.

61

Sam watched from a rooftop across the street as his target picked the lock of apartment 4B and slipped inside. Sam turned his focus to the net-book perched on the roof ledge and typed in the unit number, looking for information on the tenant registered at the address.

A moment later the renters file popped up. It seemed the unit in question belonged to one Pamela Walsh. With a few quick key strokes Sam had her DC driver's license photo along with any other information they had on file for Miss Walsh. Pamela it seemed was a local investigative reporter with aspirations of making anchor.

What did Kadar want with her? Sam wondered. He turned his attention to the photo and felt a spark of desire.

To say Miss Walsh was beautiful was an understatement, the reporter was blonde with eyes the color of whiskey. A man could get drunk from looking in those eyes too long Sam mused. She wore a black blazer over a red silk blouse, a few of the buttons were open providing just a hint of cleavage. Her mouth was curved into a wicked smile. Her lips dyed to match her top drew a man's attention. They were full and tempting they had definite potential to be labeled DSL's.

Sam drew his attention away from the photo and turned it back to the apartment building across the way. He cursed as he spotted the woman in question headed up the steps outside the building. Their Intel had suggested Miss Walsh would not be home for several hours but it seemed that something had changed because there she was in the flesh and unless he moved fast she'd walk in on Kadar's burglary and quite possibly end up one of his victims.

Sam climbed over the rooftop edge dropping down onto the fire escape. He slid down the ladder having no time for the rungs and raced across the street. "Miss Walsh," he shouted hoping to catch her before she stepped inside.

He watched as the lovely blonde turned and eyed him with question. A blond eyebrow lifted as she studied him, trying to determine if she knew him. "Yes?" She asked a hint of irritation in her voice.

"Sam Abrams from the Washington Post."

"Abrams... Oh right the war correspondent. How's the local beat treating you? I hope you're not too bored."

"Can't complain," Sam replied.

"How can I help you Mr. Abrams?"

"I heard you were looking for a sexy story to put you at the big desk, thought we might talk about it."

"Really? If you wanted to talk shop Mr. Abrams you'd have contacted me at the office instead of turning up on my private door step. So, I'll ask you again; what do you want?"

"I got a tip, someone was going to break into your place tonight," Sam blurted out running the best interference move he could think of.

"Damn it, I knew I should have moved my notes to another site," Pamela muttered as she opened the front door.

"Miss Walsh..." Sam called trying to halt her again.

"Are you coming or not," she asked annoyed.

Sam moved up the steps putting himself ahead of her, taking her keys. "What are you working on that has someone breaking in?" He asked as the stepped onto the elevator.

"You think I'm going to share with you Sam. You're cute but not that cute. It's my story."

"Is it worth your life?" Sam challenged.

"Tell you what you tell me what you're on that has you getting a tip regarding my place being broken into and I'll tell you about mine," Pamela murmured as she fixed her hair.

Sam blinked as the smell of her perfume wrapped around him. Those whiskey eyes were locked with his in challenge and he felt his groin tighten as her close proximity got to him. "Possible terrorists in DC," Sam stated hoping to scare her. Instead those intoxicating eyes lit with interest and she bit her lower lip not in nerves but excitement. Sam repressed a groan as he struggled to resist the impulse to taste that bewitching mouth for himself.

"I'm following a serial killer," Pamela stated. "If you're contact said I was being targeted then that would mean my killer is connected to your terrorists."

"Maybe," Sam corrected as the elevator dinged, signaling they reached her floor.

Sam stepped out into the hall, careful to keep Miss Walsh behind him. If bullets started flying he was going to ensure that she wasn't caught in the cross hairs.

62

"Which one's yours?" Sam questioned, careful to appear unaware of the answer. It wouldn't look good if he knew where she lived.

"4B." Pamela breathed from behind him.

Sam approached the door with caution aware Kadar could come out at any moment. He slid the key into Pamela's front door and turned it slowly. He pushed open the door allowing it to make noise announcing their arrival to the intruder, hoping to run him off before Miss Walsh saw him.

In the living room ahead of them books littered the floor having been pulled off the shelves. Sam's efforts to put himself between the civilian and the assassin went up in smoke when her whiskey colored eyes got a look at the mess. She was around him and charging down the hall toward presumably her office.

Sam raced after her. He attempted to grab her by the arm but she shrugged him off as she tore open the door. Sam's eyes settled on Kadar Handle for a split second. He saw the glint of metal as the assassin raised his gun. Sam drew Pamela back from the doorway trapping her body between his own as a silenced bullet whizzed by them.

Sam drew his own gun from his jacket and returned fire creating cover as he dragged Miss Walsh back down the hall and out of the apartment. He bypassed the elevator opting for the steps knowing he had to get her clear of the building. She'd seen his face, the assassin would not rest now until she was dead. As they hit the street Sam put his gun away and shoved Miss Walsh in the passenger seat of his car.

He rounded the hood of the car as Kadar hit the street behind them. The assassin fired at him once shattering his car mirror as he ducked into the car. Sam started the engine and pulled away from the curb speeding off into DC traffic.

"You okay?" he questioned once they were clear.

Pamela nodded. "Who are you Sam?" She questioned shaken by the encounter, he'd handled it well. Like a pro even.

"Ex-military." He replied.

"Who was that guy?"

"Looked like a hired gun," Sam stated not answering her directly but providing her with enough to satisfy her.

"Where are we going?"

"My place, it'll be safe for now."

"My notes," Pamela questioned.

"Are gone you can't go back there, he'll be waiting."

"Shit."

"I'm sorry."

"Don't be you saved my life," Pamela said grateful.

"We're not out of this yet."

"What are we going to do?"

"I'm going to start by seeing if your hunch is right, this killer of yours has connections to my terrorist piece. I'll need to know everything you can tell me about the case."

"I'll put you in touch with my contact, detective Roman. He's a friend," Pamela assured him before drawing a deep breath.

Sam pulled the black Audi A8 into his buildings parking garage. He turned off the motor and then checked his mirrors to verify they were alone. Sam unfastened his seatbelt then drew a calming breath as the adrenaline running through him demanded he move. The smell of her perfume filled his lungs for a second time and he turned to look at her.

As his eyes settled on his passenger she licked her upper lip in a display of nervousness. Heart pounding; his system over stimulated Sam reached across the seat. With a deft move he had her out of her seatbelt and pulled against him.

Whiskey eyes widened, both startled and aroused as his mouth collided with hers, tasting those bewitching lips that had been tempting him since he saw her photo, the spark of desire between them ignited setting off a powder keg as they kissed. Her mouth came alive beneath his as her nails tore at his shirt seeking skin.

Sam groaned at the feel of her pressed against him, her mouth hot and eager, hands wrapped about the length of him before she freed him of his jeans. He told himself they were in his car in the open, but couldn't find the will to care.

Sam who prided himself for his patience found he had none. He wanted her naked and writhing in pleasure as he filled her and he wanted it now. Reason gone Sam took hold of her blouse and pulled. Threads snapped as dainty buttons popped and scattered. His mouth left hers as he buried his face in her chest tasting it through the black lacy bra.

Pamela gasped, overwhelmed as she lost herself in his wild embrace. She bunched her skirt up on her hips giving him all that he silently demanded without question.

Sam ripped the matching scrap of lace between her legs as he pulled her onto him filling her depths with the proof of his insane desire. She cried out with delight and when she was ready the two began to move racing toward completion.

63

Sam blinked as he drew back from the memory and cursed to find that yet again it left him hard and hungry for her. The woman had driven him mad from the start. He should have known then that they were headed for trouble, but he'd never been able to think too clearly where Pamela was concerned.

"I wonder how she'll take the news I'm unemployed," Sam muttered as he climbed out of the car. He made his way through the lot and over to the elevator as he had that night with her six months earlier and wished that when he got upstairs she'd be waiting but knew that wasn't the case. She'd be at work for another couple hours yet. So he'd be alone with his thoughts till then.

Once he'd gotten her upstairs that night he'd tucked her safely into his bed and after securing the place, drove back to her apartment to collect his abandoned equipment. He'd then driven over to the police station to speak with Miss Walsh's friend Detective Roman.

Sam sighed; he'd not liked Lance Roman at first glance. The red haired, blue eyed cop; Sam figured most women would have counted as handsome, and the idea of Pamela hanging around him didn't sit well.

His jealousy had proved unfounded as Lance Roman only had eyes for his partner Dana Murphy but when Sam mentioned Pamela and the break in the homicide cop had seemed concerned. Sam had explained that Pamela was concerned the break in was connected to his serial killer and had requested details.

Lance had proven to be a smart man, rather than answer him he'd called Pamela and confirmed Sam's story before relating the details. Sam considered the matter but saw no direct link between her story and his assignment. Something must have shown on his face because Lance had demanded to know who he really was. Since his mandate dictated inner-departmental cooperation Sam had answered the question and advised the detective to watch his back before turning and leaving, returning to his apartment.

Upon arriving home he'd found Pamela waiting for him.

64 9 MONTHS EARLIER

"You've got a lot of nerve Mr. Abrams, you show up uninvited on my doorstep drag me about by the arm like a child, then manhandle me as if you own me before you fuck me brainless in your car and then have the audacity to leave me behind while you interview my contact. How dare you?"

"You don't have a shirt Miss Walsh," Sam reminded as he crossed the living room floor to stand at her side.

"And whose fault is that Sam?" She asked annoyed.

"Mine I suppose," he said with a cocky smirk. His blue eyes moved from her whiskey eyes to her kiss swollen lips.

"Oh you're a real piece of work, big guy, but that doesn't give you the right to cut me out of my own story," Pamela warned.

"It wasn't my intent to Miss Walsh. You were sleeping, I didn't want to disturb you. I had something to finish up and while I was out I decided to have a word with your cop."

"Next time you go nowhere without me Mr. Abrams," she demanded.

Sam wanted to argue, aware her life was at risk but could see from the look in her eyes she'd not listen. "Agreed," he relented as he eyed her with interest, the white blouse had been replaced with one of his dress-shirts. "Making yourself at home I see," he said amused and absurdly pleased. Her blonde hair was once more styled to perfection not a strand out of place. He felt an itch to bury his hands in the long length and muss it up again as he kissed her pretty mouth.

"I wasn't about to sit around here in only a wet bra and skirt," she muttered, her voice hinted at temper.

"Why not, you looked good that way, besides it's not like I'm expecting anyone."

"Just because I let you put your hands on me before Mr. Abrams that doesn't mean I will again," she hissed.

"And what makes you think I want to?" Sam asked amused.

Pamela blinked. "You don't?" she asked confused her eyes held hurt.

Sam laughed, unable to help himself, before he kissed her awakening a storm within them. When he drew back to breathe he answered her. "I didn't say that, I simply asked why you think I want to," Sam corrected.

"You're infuriating!"

"And you're sexy, legs, but I think there are other things we should be discussing before I reclaim my stolen property," Sam stated.

"What?"

"You're wearing my shirt. You didn't ask, I intend to get it back Miss Walsh and I'd rather not have to have you arrested to get it," Sam teased.

65

Sam groaned as he drew his mind away from the memory. He poured himself three fingers of whiskey and took a drink as he drew his mind away from the woman and back on track. The assignment. Yes their meeting had marked the beginning of the end but the final nail had been driven into the coffin by Kadar himself. Sam took another sip of his drink as he remembered the event that had led to Kadar's escape and his cover being blown.

He could see it as clearly as if it had happened just yesterday. He'd captured Kadar as planned. The man was in custody and he'd been excited because he'd finished his assignment, relieved because with Kadar in custody Miss Walsh's life was no longer in jeopardy and anxious, he'd soon have to start phase two of his assignment and that meant leaving the States again, leaving Pamela.

Since their tryst in the car the two had been inseparable. They're love making was hot and heavy, and thanks to his cover they shared a lot of common ground. Sam wasn't thrilled with the idea of leaving. He'd understood there was a real chance he'd lose her. So he'd done the only thing he'd known to do. He'd called her and told her Kadar was in custody and that he'd be home in an hour, he was just putting the article to bed. In truth he'd been out shopping.

Sam had bought a bottle of her favorite wine and a ring. He knew even then that it was a bit fast to propose, they'd only known each other a few months but he'd fallen hard for her and he didn't want her to go. He'd made plans as he went for the night looking forward to seeing her. All his planning couldn't have prepared him for the nightmare he faced that night.

66 6 MONTHS EARLIER

Sam stepped off the elevator on his floor a bottle of wine in his left hand as he fished his keys out of his pocket. His feet carried him towards the apartment, his eyes not really focused on his surroundings, he's lost in his plans for the evening. The ring in his pocket weighed heavy on his mind.

Was he being foolish to ask her? After all they'd only met three months earlier.

What if she said no? What if she said yes? Was he really ready for this; he asked himself? Before he could come up with a response Sam noticed the door. It hung open half way, the door frame splintered. The bottle of wine he held fell from numb fingers and shattered on the marble floor, it contents spraying him, staining his jeans.

As the initial shock wore off, instinct took over. Sam drew his gun from inside his jacket and entered the apartment with caution.

Inside there were signs of a struggle but no one moved. Fear seized him and panic set in; caution was thrown out, as he rushed about the place searching for her. Images of her dead or bleeding, dying; filled his mind and he shoved them aside. His search proved fruitless she's not here. The knowledge she'd been taken was just starting to sink in as his phone rang.

Sam re-holstered his gun; before picking up the offending object off the counter. "Hello."

"Hello Mr. Abrams I trust you've realized by now that your pretty reporter friend is missing. I have her. She is alive at this moment and relatively unharmed. If you wish her to remain so you will aid me in freeing my man Kadar Handle." A sinister voice hissed through the phone.

"When I find you York…"

"Ah, but you won't Mr. Abrams and you're wasting time. You

have 24 hours to get him out of the country. un-followed or Miss Walsh will end up as the Fury Killer's next victim. It's such a terrible way to die; I wouldn't wish it on any woman but I imagine you already know what that means, so, if you still wish to give that ring in your pocket to your sexy housemate while she's breathing I suggest you get started."

"I want proof she's alive," Sam demanded forcing himself to focus, knowing if he didn't that Pamela would die.

"One hour." Mr. York responded before the phone clicked ending the call.

Sam roared in rage as he threw the phone across the room in a display of temper. The offensive object that had carried such cursed news broke as it hit the wall. Sam blew out a breath trying to calm down. If he was going to help Pamela he had to stay in control. Pulling his cell phone out of his pocket he punched in the number for his handler and waited for an answer.

"Mr. Abrams?" the voice on the other end questioned.

"I have a problem."

67 WASHINGTON DC, VIRGINIA
FRIDAY
3PM

The proof York had sent was live video feed directly to his laptop of Pamela in a sound proof room in front of a black back drop so that he'd have no detail to follow to find her. When the video stopped he'd been given a reminder of how many hours were left to complete the task of getting Kadar Handel out of the country.

He'd cursed once more before putting a plan together to get the other man out. After speaking to his handler it was clear that he was on his own with this. Kadar was too dangerous a threat to the nation to allow him to go free over one woman. Sam realized now he'd felt betrayed that day. He'd done everything the Agency had ever asked of him without question and the one time he asked for something in return they'd refused him.

Sam had arranged for an interrogation with Kadar and required transport of the prisoner to a supposed target location. Once they were outside the Company's walls he'd taken steps to ensure Kadar's escort was out of the way, then using private contacts had smuggled the other man out of the country. He figured the Company was aware he was behind the escape but for their part they remained silent.
Sam had kept an ace up his sleeve in case they came after him. He alone was going to know where to locate Kadar for pick up. He'd been careful to keep a man on the terrorist but no one connected to the Agency. While he was willing to let the prisoner go to keep Pamela alive, he was not willing to let him vanish. The man was in the wind but not for long.
Sam's phone rang approximately fourteen hours after Kadar boarded the cargo plane bound for Bagdad. He figured that meant the other man had arrived safely and York was aware the task he'd given him was complete.

"Hello."

"Well done Mr. Abrams, I'm impressed. Your lady is waiting for you at Studio Theatre on 14th street."

Sam didn't respond, he simply hung up the call and ran out of the apartment headed for the garage. He was in his Audi and on the move in a matter of moments. The ride over was a blur, he was aware, he sped across town but had no idea how he actually got there, it was as if he'd blinked and was in the building.

He found her bound and gagged in the old prop room. Alive and basically unharmed save for a bump on the head. In two strides he was across the room and had her in his arms. Hazel eyes filled with relief as tears dripped from tired eyes.

"Shh, I've got you it's all over, your safe now," he assured her as he worked at freeing her.

When her arms were loose she wrapped them around his neck and kissed him. "Sam."

"Did you see who took you?" Sam questioned realizing she may just have seen York.

"No he was wearing all black his face hidden by a ski mask," Pamela said frustrated.

"Don't worry about it. It's not important. I'm just glad you're okay," he breathed as he kissed her forehead. "Come on, let's get you out of here," Sam murmured as he picked her up and carried her out to his waiting car.

He'd taken her to a hotel and tended to her needs. Taking care of the small cut on her brow from the struggle when she was taken, feeding her and helping her to settle in. In the heat of the moment he'd asked her to marry him and she'd agreed. As Sam sipped his whiskey he wondered again how York had managed to get to her. He'd been careful not to let anyone know where she was staying. Made it clear to her, she could not call anyone or use a computer.

Despite his precautions the man had found her; not only that, he'd gotten past his nearly unbeatable security system. Doubt gnawed at the back of his mind but he pushed it aside by reasoning the other man had been watching him probably for months. After all he'd known that Sam had bought the ring that day. He'd had his cell number. the means to connect to his secure laptop. He wondered now if the whole thing with Kadar had been York testing his skills for some unknown reason.

Sam sighed what did it matter now? He was done. He'd never have to think about York or Kadar again. He was a simple law abiding citizen again. He'd traded his career for Pamela and now that he'd had a little bit of time to think on it he had to question if he'd made the right choice. Since they'd married she'd changed.

The spontaneous wild woman he'd met was now a ghost he rarely saw. They were like ships passing at night. He was busy with work and she as well. Her career was her primary interest. The passion between them had cooled some too. Not that they didn't still have the occasional heated encounter but it seemed empty. Like he wasn't connecting with her on an emotional level just physical.

Sam drew a breath as he looked at their wedding photo. He was over analyzing things; she still loved him, he assured himself as he finished off his first glass and poured a second. He took a seat on the couch to wait for her. His thoughts turning to the future. Now that he was unemployed. what was he going to do with his life, Sam wondered. He was just beginning to contemplate the matter when the phone rang.

Sam got to his feet and crossed the floor to the kitchen counter where the cordless phone sat in the cradle recharging. "Ello," he said dropping the h due to the alcohol in his system. He realized then he should probably not be drinking on an empty stomach.

"Damn it Sam are you drunk?" Pamela's voice questioned from the other end. It sizzled with annoyance.

"A little," he said with a shrug. "When you comin' home legs?"

"Perhaps, when you sober up. I just heard a disturbing rumor that you were fired from the paper for a fraudulent story. Since your home and drunk I assume it's true."

"Yeah, they let me go," Sam confirmed.

"Of all the dumb shit things to do Sam Abrams this was the worst. Do you realize that my reputation as a reporter is connected to yours? I could lose everything I've worked for because of this; you jack ass. Damn you Sam I'm sick of your selfish and self-destructive behavior. You're not the same man I married. I want a divorce."

Sam blinked as the harsh words hit him hard; going a considerable ways towards sobering him up. "Pamela you can't mean that. I love you and you love me and this thing with the paper is a huge misunderstanding it will blow over," Sam assured her. "Please sweetie, don't do this to us," Sam requested.

"Don't you sweetie me Sam Abrams, it's not going to change my mind. I don't know what you did but it's not going to just blow over. I heard the producer on the phone. You've been black listed. you'll never work as a reporter again. I may lose the anchor spot over this. How could you?"

"I didn't think…"

"That's right you didn't and that's the problem. I won't lose my career for you Sam. We have great sex and some stimulating conversation but that's not enough. We're through." Pamela said before she hung up.

Sam set the phone back in the charger. his ears ringing with her rejection. His heart pounded in his chest wildly and rage built inside him. The stupid bitch, he'd given up his career with the paper and the Agency to save her and this was how she responded, no sympathy, no questions as to why she just dropped him like a bad habit. His heart ached with the betrayal and the loss. He'd really screwed up, Sam realized. He looked to the glass of whiskey in his hand and disgusted threw it against the wall.

Drinking was not going to numb the pain nor was it going to solve his problems. Taking out his company phone which he still needed to return, he dialed the number for his handler.

"Hey it's me, I want to be relocated."

"Where to?"

"As far from DC as you can get me," Sam muttered.

"What's up?"

"Pamela is leaving me. She wants a divorce."

"Damn that's rough end of a marriage and a career. I've got an opening in Vegas."

"I'll take it."

"How soon?"

"As soon as the divorce is finalized."

"Sam for what it's worth I'm sorry, did you want me to inform…"

"No I'm done. Do you know who burned me or why?"

"Afraid not."

"It doesn't matter. This chapter of my life is over."

"Good luck Mr. Abrams."

"Thanks," Sam said with a sign before he hung up the phone. As he packed his things he wondered if Vegas would be far enough away from DC to escape from Pamela and his grave mistake. He wasn't sure but he was sure as hell going to find out.

If you enjoyed DISCOVERING TRUTH then check out these other titles in the *MANTLE OF THE GODS SERIES.*

Here's a sample From *QUEST FOR TRUTH.*

1

"I'm taking a few days off."

The words echoed in her mind as Anna burst through the door of her hotel suite. It hit the wall with a bang then slammed behind her. Startled, Anna jumped. She turned, expecting the enemy at her back. Finding no one Anna let out a deep breath, she'd been unaware of holding. She was alone.

"Get a grip Anna. They don't know your intentions…yet. It won't take them long to figure it out though," she muttered to herself. After a momentary pause, she steadied herself. Willing her racing pulse to subside, she sighed again. Surveying her spacious junior suite almost like it was the first time; soft green wallpaper was complemented by sensible dark wood furniture. A queen-sized bed covered in a white with a strip of golden damask fabric running along the foot of the bed. A few of the traditional landscape-style portraits lined the walls. Her desk was piled high with electronic gadgets, her computer, and specialty tools the only sign of her presence in the room. It was neat – tidy. Just the way she liked it.

"Better get moving, girl." She ordered her stiff legs to respond. Knowing she was about to swath a path of destruction through the space – already regretting it.

With determined strides, she threw open the closet door. Reaching inside, she pushed the clothes hanging crisp and pressed on the hangers into two groups. Organized by color and style, she wrapped her tanned arms around the first bundle. Heaving them off the metal rod then throwing them on the bed. She repeated the process with the second bundle and moved onto the shoes. Grabbing them up by pairs and tossing them beside the clothes.

Closet emptied, she spun on her heels; raced for the dresser.

Pulling open; the top drawer then filling her grip with neatly laid out undergarments and a couple of silk nightgowns. She tossed them into the clothing pile. Slammed the top drawer shut, almost catching her fingers. She yelped. Yanked her hand back, glaring at the offending inanimate object.

Then she hauled open the second drawer, seizing her socks and tank tops, before removing her shorts and work pants from the bottom drawer. With her hands full, she turned; strode to the bed, dumping them into the pile then charged into the bathroom.

Pulling open one of the storage drawers in the sterile-looking off-white bathroom, she grabbed her travel bag; unzipped it. She swept all her toiletries and makeup into the case, tugging the zipper closed. She pitched it out the bathroom door onto the bed. Anna contemplated grabbing her personal travel shampoo bottles and soap. She thought better of it. They'd ooze out onto her other stuff since she didn't have time to put them away properly.

She hurried over to the desk, near the flat panel T.V. The dark semi-reflective surface capturing her harried look and disheveled clothes. She groaned turning her focus from the surface. The screen sat perched like a sentinel guarding the room; reminding her of the endless stare of some black-eyed creature. Anna thought of little green men and other oddities that didn't exist. She shook her head with disgust. She'd been contemplating such peculiar things far too often of late.

Snatching her black purse from the back of the chair, she dug for her keys; then threw the bag absently onto the dresser beside the television. She crammed her keys in her pants pocket. Racing back to the closet, she dragged out her suitcases and luggage cart; wrangling both up next to the bed.

Anna cringed. Looking at the pile on the bed made her uneasy. The tops of the hangers twisted and curled at odd angles like tangled claws. Suits and other apparel formed the long curved lines of limbs and a body. The clear plastic makeup bag and black purse resembled a disembodied eye and mouth.

"It looks like some weird monster," she said; disgusted by the tousled mess and the strange beast lurking therein. Her skin crawled. Her thoughts wandering back to her work. The implications of what she'd unearthed made her palms sweat. "No time for that now," she chastised herself. "Slay this beast first."

Even as she attacked the pile, stuffing clothes into the suitcase, she grimaced at the thought of having to undo this destruction whenever she did make it home. Everything would have to be sent off to the dry cleaners again to be pressed…She hadn't even worn half of these clothes. What a waste! Fear lingered in her belly; threatening to turn the small shiver within into a wracking shudder. Dropping her travel case atop the pile, she stomped the items down with her foot. Wrestling the zipper closed on the hunter green suitcase. She lugged the heavy bag upright, bumping the thick leather corners against her shins. She cried out in pain. The suitcase was designed to take a severe beating in transit—her legs were not.

Packing in haste was not something she was accustomed to. Given the mounting situation she didn't want to stick around too much longer. "Find a safe place. Gather your thoughts. Make sense of all this madness," she told herself for the hundredth time.

Anna turned her attention to her workstation and groaned—the last bastion of organization was about to be thwarted. Here haste was more problematic. Items could be too easily damaged, but she had to find a way to make it quick. Reaching for her smaller suitcase, she set it on the dresser next to the desk, flipping back the top. She steadied herself then began packing her workspace with a sigh. If her employers found out what she was up to she'd be going nowhere.

Frustration hit her. She slammed her palm down on the desk. "Damn it! This isn't fair. I shouldn't have to go. It was bad enough they pushed me out of my work at the main site – now this. If it weren't for me, there wouldn't even be a site," Anna grumbled with frustration. She mashed a button; shutting down her laptop. Taking hold of the annoyance and letting it drive her she jerked the cables from wall and machine. Wrapping them up, cinching Velcro ties. She placed small electronic items in their protective cases. Anna slipped her laptop into its padded sleeve in the top of the suitcase. Locking it in place then loaded her camera and the other tools. Each was tucked away in its specific place.

Her gaze fell on her field kit. The soft roll of well-worn camel-colored canvas perched on the far side of the desk. She picked up the kit, feeling the familiar weight of picking and cleaning tools. The soft clang of the tools contained within gave her an odd sense of peace. She placed it gently inside the suitcase. Her hand lingered for a moment on the fabric. How long would it be before she came back? That didn't matter right now. Just focus, she told herself.

Anna turned back to the desk, looking over the scattered paper items and small miscellaneous objects. She grabbed the suitcase, placed it in the seat of the desk chair. Shut her eyes then swept the remaining items into the bag. An assortment of note books, sketch pads, journals, pens, pencils and photos fell into the bag with a clatter. Anna's eyes popped open. She nearly wept at the sight before her.

She loved her work. It pained her to mistreat any of it. Discovering secrets from the past was her obsession. She was a truth-seeker, wherever it led. It was making the fact she was leaving her dig difficult. It can't be helped, she told herself. I've seen things I cannot explain. Why won't they listen to me? There must be a reasonable explanation for what we found. How could they shut me out?

Anna had to get away. Gain some perspective. Ground herself again in truth. She blinked; now wasn't the time to rehash her reasons for going. She needed to finish packing. Get out of there, now.

Anna moved to the bed and dropped to her knees. Pulling the blanket up, she reached under. Her fingers brushed against cool wood. Having located the most important of her possessions, her grip tightened. She pulled the smooth cigar box to her. She shuddered as she moved it afraid to disturb it too much. The contents within were worth more than anything she owned. She'd wrapped the item within to the best of her ability. Still she worried it wouldn't be enough. This wasn't protocol for transporting a priceless antique. However, she couldn't have her little clandestine act discovered. Anything crated would normally be photographed, coded, and properly cataloged. The contents within the box had not. If her employers knew what it contained, she'd be in more trouble than she cared to consider.

Anna piled her suitcases onto the hand cart, stacking the larger one first; topped by the second. She pulled a canvas carrying tote out of a suitcase pocket. Wrapped the cigar box in the tote and added the package to the cart. Tacking everything down with cord to ensure nothing fell off. She shouldered her purse; then grabbed the handle for the dolly. Anna took one final survey of the room to ensure she hadn't missed anything. Satisfied, she opened the door leading into the main hall of the hotel.

2

Anna peered down the passageway in both directions certain someone would be waiting to spring on her. She entered the hall; relieved to find no one else there. Anna walked at a fast clip down the corridor to the elevator. Her heels thudded a faint sound on the patterned carpet. The wheels of her cart squealed behind her drowning out her foot falls. At the end of the hall, facing the antique-white metal elevator doors, Anna pressed the down-arrow. She waited. Her foot tamped in a show of impatience as the elevator groaned, responding to the call. Nothing like foreign hotels, she thought glibly. She contemplated taking the stairs, but then thought better of it. Besides she was carrying precious cargo, how would she get the cart downstairs without a total disaster?

While she stood, she considered her next move. Once she got back to the states, she wouldn't be able to stay at home for long. They would come looking for her. She'd go elsewhere, but where? Family was out of the question. That'd be the first place the company would go looking for her. Anna shoved the matter aside as the elevator dinged announcing it's coming arrival. She'd cross that bridge when she came to it. Besides, she'd have plenty of time to figure it out on the airplane. Not like she would be sleeping anyway.

The doors of the elevator slid open. Anna hurried inside. She pressed the button for the garage then focused on turning the bulky cart around inside the small space. After a few moments of struggle, she managed to get it facing forward, as the elevator descended. An errant sleeve had spilled out between the zippers of her suitcase. She muttered a curse.

"Is it pinched in the zipper? Oh no! I love this blouse," she sighed, exasperated. Anna shoved the sleeve back inside, closed the bag. Then inspected the other bags making sure nothing else was hanging out. Seeing not a thing out of place, she turned to her reflection in the glass, and smoothed out her hair. She rubbed at the small shadow of mascara under her eyes and realized it was dark circles, edged with obvious lines of stress. Anna tried to relax. She had to look normal, put together, ordered. Otherwise the wrong people might take notice of her unusual behavior.

"Breathe Anna," she murmured. The doors opened in the parking garage. Anna looked out at the gloomy grey lot with distrust. It didn't look very inviting or friendly for that matter. She took a step forward and stopped, glancing around ill at ease.

"Perfect, Anna. You just had to watch that stupid psychological horror flick last night with the woman who got attacked in the parking garage. When will you learn? How long after the last one were you afraid to take a shower?" Anna felt her heart race. Her lungs tightened as shadows deepened. Seeming to grow, sprouting to life in the dark corridors of the concrete garage. Panic swept over her like a tidal wave. Her feet wouldn't respond, though she knew she should walk forward. "I can't do this," she breathed.

The open elevator buzzed; a loud and annoying sound of protest at being left ajar too long. Anna cursed. The noise startled her out of her frozen state. If anyone was out there she'd just let them know where she was. The new jolt in her nerves propelled her forward. She set off at a rapid pace towards her car. Looking around to make sure no one would see her hurrying with so much, luggage in tow. The echo of her boot heels clacked on the concrete floor, which only served to amplify the squealing cart racket and garner her sense of urgency.

Car doors opened and closed, engines roared to life in the distance. Patrons came and went about their daily lives, oblivious to her newly discovered truth...something that would change what the world believed in. How can humanity not know? How could her employers hide something this important? A huge scientific discovery and they wanted to muzzle her. They had excommunicated her from her site; tossed her back to do dredge work. It was insulting!

She shook her head clearing her thoughts; allowing the frustration to fuel her. Chasing away her anxieties; seeing the navy blue rental car parked another thirty feet in front of her Anna slowed her pace. Someone's car alarm beeped nearby. She jumped then hurried on. Anna pressed the car remote, popping the trunk. Reaching the rental Anna tried to catch her breath. She loaded up the trunk, taking care not to jostle the items in the smaller bags too much.

Anna slumped into the driver's seat, started the ignition and drove around to the main entrance. She looked about her for suspicious cars or people. Saw only tourists and tired travelers.

She put the car in park but left it idling in front of the main glass doors of the King David Hotel. Stepping out of the car she walked into the lobby; heading straight for the front desk clerk with purpose. Anna was careful steeling her nerves; putting on her normal aura of being in control. The clerk spotted her and smiled.

"Ah, Miss Gallagher, good evening, how may I help you?" Liam's smile was genuine. Anna had always liked him.

"Hi, I…" Anna searched her mind trying to draw back the plan. Why was she there? The room keys in her pocket burned in her mind. The reflex of returning the plastic items to their rightful owners hit her with some demand. "Stick to the plan, Anna," she thought to herself.

"Miss Gallagher?"

"Oh sorry, I wanted to say don't worry about the fresh towels. The ones I have are fine. I don't need them changed."

"Are you certain? I apologize that you have had issues with the maid not changing them out the last couple of days." His accent was thick, but his English was well-spoken. She had appreciated the fact that most Israelis did speak some English while she was learning her Hebrew.

"No, no, its fine – todah."

"Of course, is there anything else we can do for you?" he asked.

"Oh, cancel my wakeup call tomorrow morning. I'm going to sleep in for once."

"I'll see to it Miss." She watched him scribble something down on a notepad then level his gaze on hers once more. She felt the flicker of concern in his eyes more than she saw it. Maybe she looked worse for wear than she thought. Anna had been told she wore her emotions on her sleeve.

"Thank you, Liam." She said before she turned and left. Once outside, the heat struck her. Thoughts of her endeavor weighed in on her once more. She hoped this little tactic would buy her some time…a couple of days at least. Like her, they were over thirteen hours away by flight. She would have at least from the time of her discovered absence until the time it took for the plane to reach D.C. before they could track her down. That was assuming they didn't discover her missing until at least tomorrow sometime. It was a lot to presume. A big gamble, but she didn't have a choice. She'd seen too much to go on ignoring it. The museum back home had to be informed.

3

Anna sat with her head resting on a small rectangular pillow pressed against the shade of the airplane window. She groaned finding yet again that she couldn't get comfortable. Giving up she switched on her light. Sleep it seemed was beyond her reach. Anna stowed the pillow. Took out a stack of newspapers she bought while at the airport in Israel. She unfolded the one on the top of the stack; began flipping through the pages. Looking for anything on the discovery near the Dead Sea.

Seeing nothing she muttered a curse. Setting the paper aside she switched to the next in the stack and moved her way through each.

"The find of the century and no one knows anything about it. How was it possible?" Anna muttered with disgust. Not one paper showed any sign of being aware of the dig. It didn't make sense. They couldn't all be bought off, could they?

"When the director of the Smithsonian sees what I have to show him that'll change."